NIGHTRIDER'S MOON

Frank Tennant's mother used to tell him no man was all bad. But Frank had seen enough to doubt his mother's adage, starting with his own uncle; Charles Burton was a wealthy rancher whose greed made him turn on his own flesh and blood. As if what Burton did to Frank's mother wasn't bad enough, he did not hesitate to send hired gunmen after Frank when Frank took back what was rightfully his.

Then Jorge Medina came to his rescue. Soon Frank discovered that most people are like himself: capable of rising to goodness—or sinking to evil . . .

NIGHTRIDER'S MOON

Lauran Paine

WESTERNS

First published 1988
by Walker Publishing Company, Inc.

This hardback edition 1992
by Chivers Press
by arrangement with
the author

ISBN 0 7451 4507 8

British Library Cataloguing in Publication Data available

All the characters and events portrayed in this story
are fictitious.

Printed and bound in Great Britain by
Redwood Press Limited, Melksham, Wiltshire

CHAPTER 1

Guadalupe

IT was not just a wind, it more closely approximated a Santa Ana, one of those howling dust storms during which shifts in wind velocity and direction were not accompanied with the usual brief lulls. It blew continuously. It raised a dust cloud tree-top-high, which seemed to be carrying away whatever topsoil there was in this country of few trees, sparse clumps of bunchgrass, searing summer sunlight, and seemingly endless miles of desert terrain.

Santa Ana winds could blow without respite for a week, occasionally longer. They cut visibility down to a yard or two. They made cattle and horses turn their rumps to the driving force of the storm, lower their heads, close their eyes, and drift; afterward, with swollen, watering eyes, they would half-heartedly search for browse and graze.

In the towns and villages, aside from carrying away parts of rooftops and forcing dun dust through crevices and beneath doors to form piles, the winds made walking across wood floors—even eating off plates and platters—a gritty experience.

Santa Anas shortened tempers, silted *acequias,* restricted movement, and piled dust like snow against the lee side of buildings, and always brought forth exasperated denunciations of a country where winds of eighty miles an hour were normal visitations, usually in late spring, but also likely to arrive in summer and autumn.

But the residents of the *tierra caliente* were rooted. Those who swore the loudest that they would not put another year in an area where it got hot enough in summer to fry eggs on rocks and cold enough in winter to ice over troughs—not to

1

mention the Santa Anas—were the same ones who were there when the next hot summer, or frigid winter, or the immobilizing winds arrived.

Mostly, the natives were descendants of people who had been there a hundred years. They had grown and matured there. And while many had been to other areas of the Southwest, or even up north through Colorado to Wyoming, Idaho, and Montana, they returned where they had roots, the *tierra caliente,* the hot country.

In the year 1835, Mexican Generalisimo Antonio Lopez de Santa Anna y Lebron had undertaken a Journey of Death across the forbidding desert, the most direct route to Texas, where he intended to crush rebellious colonists. He started forth with eight thousand people. When he arrived in Texas, he had six thousand. Wind, rain, snow, starvation, lack of adequate water, and desertion had accounted for the disparity. It was the huge dust cloud arising over his straggling column, visible for miles and whipped by desert winds, that provided the name for the much later dust and wind storms of the Southwest. The Santa Ana wind.

It was a poor country. Life for four-legged and two-legged creatures was a struggle for existence in a land whose top three or four inches of leached-out soil provided a bare minimum for those who were required to live off it, which meant more than two-thirds of the native population.

There were a few cities, many villages, and countless hamlets. Mostly, as with the village of Guadalupe, the latest conquerors of the Southwest controlled the commerce, owned nearly all the buildings and businesses that lined Guadalupe's main thoroughfare, and were responsible for the importation of items gringos thought were necessary, and the Mexicans, who lived behind Main Street in their historic mud-wattle residences, considered unobtainable luxuries.

For many years the rift between newcomers and natives had been steadily widening until, as Guadalupe's lawman

Marshal Cord Bierk said, "It's more than the language, it's the Mexican's customs and his everlastin' resignation. He don't even cuss the Santa Anas. It don't matter to him that stagecoaches can't run, freighters got to hole up, commerce comes to a standstill."

Bud Shilling, who operated the harness works in Guadalupe, a burly, graying man with squinty eyes and a dragoon mustache stained a uniform mahogany color from chewing tobacco, listened to the wind in the roadway for a moment, then leaned against Will Perkins's bar and said, "You know that old man who works for me, George Medina?"

Marshal Bierk nodded and looked at the empty jolt glass in front of his big hand. "Yeah."

"Well now, Cord, him and me discussed this very thing a lot of times."

Marshal Bierk turned a face of coarse features. "An' he's got the answer, Bud?"

Shilling straightened up long enough to fish forth his chewing plug, then leaned on the counter again. "Seems likely, Cord. He says Mexicans see it different than we do. Old George says long before we arrived, damned In'ians ruled the whole country, even partway down into Mexico. He told me that when he was a youngster, folks forted up at night, and real often when they come out in the morning, their livestock was gone. Then the Mexicans come with soldiers, and he said they wasn't much better'n the In'ians. After the Mexicans got run out by us, then came the *norteamericano* freighters, stockmen, merchants, an' we took over their country, towns and all."

Cord Bierk exchanged a look with Perkins the saloonman, who was listening while drying glasses with a soggy towel. Bierk winked, and Will Perkins almost smiled back.

Bud continued. "Now then, George says, who'll come after us, and what possible difference will it make?" Bud straightened up off the bar. "That's their outlook. They've been through it all many times before. There's nothing they can do about most of it, so they get by, raise a few vegetables, herd their goats, make their likker, go to the Mission on Sunday, and don't see much point in killin' themselves workin'."

Marshal Bierk grunted, slapped a silver coin beside his empty jolt glass, and was turning toward the roadway door when he said, "Bud, they're lazy and shiftless. I guess Medina gave you the excuse for them shortcomings, but he sure as hell didn't give you the reason for them. Mexicans are just plain lazy."

After Cord Bierk had left, Will Perkins finished with the jolt glasses and made a wide sweep of his bartop with his soggy towel, then grinned at the saddle and harness maker. "I used to think that when Cord's been in this country as long as I have, he'd change."

Shilling worried off a corner of his plug and tongued it into his cheek before speaking. "And what do you think now?"

Perkins chuckled as he draped the soiled towel from a peg below the bar. "I think any gringo who stays down here on the South Desert is either crazy or is afraid to go back up to civilization because maybe some U.S. marshal'll grab him."

Bud thoughtfully chewed while eyeing the saloonman. Eventually he asked a question. "Are you putting those labels on Cord Bierk—he's either crazy or a fugitive?"

Perkins, who was a turkey-necked, pale-eyed, thin man in his late fifties, an amiable individual who had been on the South Desert fifteen years and no one knew any more about him now than the first month he was in Guadalupe, gazed at the harness maker with a whimsical look. "I don't put labels on folks, Bud. Leastways not out loud. Naw, I figure that Cord's got bad nerves from the Santa Ana."

Shilling paid for his jolt, and as he was doing this he said, "Who hasn't?" and left the saloon.

That was the last day of the wind storm. The next morning the sky was clear blue and flawless, the sun brought springtime warmth, and the only visible signs of the defunct Santa Ana were the residue of drifts of wind-driven earth against buildings and some rooftops partially denuded. With the Santa Ana dead, life—human and other forms—could begin shaking off its effects.

In Guadalupe there was some sweeping up and digging out to be done, which took about three days. But beyond town, where cattlemen always had trouble keeping track of their animals anyway, it would be weeks before all the saddle-backing had been completed, cattle brought back to their home ranges, and the tallies of losses were completed.

Springtime on the South Desert was brief in comparison to the other seasons of the year, but it was also the best time; grass appeared, flowers blossomed where there were dusty, thorny bushes, days were warm without being hot, and on full-moon nights there was a fragrance carried for miles by warm, soft breezes.

In Guadalupe's Mex town, young rutting bucks serenaded, their songs invariably having to do with injustice, death, oppression, and poverty, reflecting the dolorous sentiment of their Anáhuac and Castile heritage.

Jorge (George) Medina's adobe house had been built by his grandfather, an army deserter. Jorge's father, also skilled with leather, had added two rooms. Jorge had added another room before his wife died, leaving him with an infant daughter. By local standards, Jorge was a success. He was a respectable individual whose skill was recognized over in Gringo town where he worked at the saddle and harness works.

The last night of the Santa Ana, when Jorge passed down one of the dogtrots between commercial buildings on Main Street and emerged in Mex town, he paused to clear his throat of gritty dust. Then he walked the remaining distance to his residence, which was near the northern end of Mex town, where it was possible to stand outside and see the ancient adobe Mission without interfering structures.

But tonight Jorge did not even glance northward. He went

directly into the house where his daughter had four candles burning, two on an old rough table, two in wall niches. She greeted him with a solemn smile and went at once to the cooking area to bring supper. But as she returned with plates, Jorge draped his old hat from a worn-smooth wooden peg in the wall and said, "Dead?"

His daughter shook her head and put supper on the table. Jorge sighed and pulled up a bench to sit on. In Spanish, which he rarely used anymore, he said, "How is it that they don't die when they should?"

His daughter's pale gold complexion showed flawlessly in the shadowy light as she sat opposite her father and replied, also in Spanish, "You have told me many times it is not possible to go until God wills it."

Jorge pulled the supper plate closer and, without looking up from it, commented dryly, "It must be very hard for God. How many men continue to survive with three bullet holes in them?" Then he raised his eyes to her lovely face. "He has had to compromise, I think, because you have worked so hard to keep this man alive."

The beautiful girl smiled. "You taught me from childhood that, for the injured, I should give from my heart."

Jorge smiled back at her. "Well, the Santa Ana wiped out his tracks and certainly held away those who probably were tracking him."

The girl's smile faded slowly. "Father, why is it that you think the worst?"

"Because . . . This is excellent stew and you are the blessed of my heart . . . But where are the jalapeños?"

"They are in the stew. Move a candle closer to find them."

He did not move the candle closer—he did not want to *see* the peppers, he wanted to *taste* them. He sighed and returned to what he had begun to say. "It is not that I think the worst—at least not always. It is because this man has been shot three times, from behind, which means he was fleeing. And there are those saddlebags with all that money in them."

"And," his daughter said dryly, "the rosary with the beautiful gold crucifix, Father."

Jorge chewed, swallowed, and reached for the cup of red wine. "Possibly from the same source as all that money."

His daughter sat back, dark eyes fixed on her father. "When we found him in the goat corral out back three days ago, you said he needed care. So we have him in the back room. *I* did not say to take him there."

"That was before we stripped him to cleanse the wounds. It was also before we opened the saddlebags."

"Good then. Now you want to tie him on his horse and take him far out somewhere."

Jorge finished eating, drained the cup and looked across at his daughter, who was now twenty-three years old and a picture-perfect image of his wife, at rest now in the Mission graveyard. They had been married only eleven years when she died. "You are very beautiful," he said, arising from the table.

She blinked in surprised silence.

He gave her no opportunity to recover because in another way she was like her mother: she would argue.

He jerked his head and went to a niche for one of the candles. "Bring another one. Let us see how this gringo with a handsome crucifix and the ivory-handled pistol with seven filings on it is managing to remain alive when as God certainly knows, such a thing should not be."

CHAPTER 2

Tennant

HIS name was Frank Tennant. He had startlingly blue eyes set in a darkly tanned face, and although he was whisker stubbled with sunken cheeks and a wide mouth held flat from suffering, his mind was clear and active. But his body beneath the light blanket showed bones where there should have been flesh.

He watched the Medinas enter his small room, which was sparsely furnished and lighted by one candle in a niche. Tennant forced a vague smile.

Jorge nodded, and in silence pulled back the blanket while Antonia held the candle for her father to examine the bandages; he grunted because obviously his daughter had already changed them recently, something he usually did himself. Jorge raised his eyebrows, and Antonia simply said, "It had to be done."

They spoke in English. Her father did not question the fact that the bandages had to be changed. He said, "I won't open them, but I wish you had waited because I want to know about infection."

Antonia lowered the candle slightly. "I didn't see any signs of it," she said.

"No swelling, discoloration, no running from the wounds, no high heat?"

She shook her head. Jorge sighed and straightened up after replacing the blanket. He met the wounded man's gaze. Jorge smiled and made a little gesture with his hands. "I don't see how," he told Frank Tennant. "When we found you, your clothes were filthy—you were lying in a corral which hasn't been cleaned in years."

Tennant's voice was softly husky. He was very ill, weak as a kitten, and listless. "It may come. Be patient, Mister Medina."

Jorge flushed. "You misunderstand. I don't want any infection. It's just that it seems almost impossible that there shouldn't be some."

Frank Tennant's stare went to the beautiful girl. "She cleans out the wounds with salt water. She does a very thorough job."

Jorge nodded. "How do you feel today?"

A shadow of wry humor showed in the darkly tanned, emaciated face as Tennant replied. "Maybe a little better than yesterday and hopefully a little worse than tomorrow."

Antonia's quick smile showed. Even her father's eyes twinkled. He said, "I'm seventy years old, *vaquero*. I have seen many men with gunshot wounds. It has seemed to me that the ones who live through are the men who have clear consciences and humor—you have the humor. Antonia, will you bring a glass of wine? Here, *dulce*, put the candle on the table."

The moment they were alone, the older man dropped down upon a three-legged stool and eyeing his uninvited guest skeptically, said, "I don't know about the clear conscience. . . ."

Frank Tennant's blue eyes were fixed upon Jorge's face for a long moment before he said, "You speak English without any accent."

After an interval of silence Jorge said, "That don't have anything to do with what we were talking about, but I was orphaned very young and three different Mission fathers raised me. They spoke English. The only time they spoke anything close to Spanish was during services. Sometimes they spoke in Latin. I've answered your question. Will you answer mine?"

Tennant eased his head around on the mattress filled with cornhusks. It rattled with even the slightest movement. He stared at the niche where candlelight wavered. "Clear conscience? I think so, Mister Medina. I don't believe I was wrong, but I reckon you could get an argument about that."

"From anyone who might arrive in Guadalupe?"

Tennant continued to watch the unsteady candlelight. "I don't know. I've been thinking about that. They wouldn't be able to follow my tracks, not after that storm. But they're not children—they know the direction I was riding in. Maybe one of these days they might arrive in Guadalupe to ask questions." He looked into Medina's face. "Antonia said neither of you has told anyone I am in your house."

Jorge conceded that curtly. "Neither of us has. But there is the horse and saddle."

Frank Tennant weakly nodded his head. "Yeah. You can hide the outfit."

"And the horse? It's branded on the left shoulder."

"I don't think they'd know that brand. I doubt that they even saw the horse."

Jorge shrugged. Tennant saw this and turned back toward the candle before speaking again.

"All right. Turn him loose. Chase him away."

Jorge wagged his head. "Stray horses always turn up some-where. In this country, stockmen would maybe find him. Or goat tenders from Mex town. The brand, señor."

Tennant was silent for a few moments. "Give him to *arrieros* going down into Mexico, or maybe up north."

Jorge considered the thin face with its strong features and sunken places. "I'll take care of the horse."

Tennant's eyes came swiftly back. "Don't shoot him."

Jorge pushed up off the stool. "No, I won't shoot him. He's a good animal." He glanced over his shoulder, but there was no one in the doorway, so he turned back as he said, "What about the saddlebags?"

"Hide them."

"That's not what I meant. Of course we'll hide them—they are full of money. I think you are a range rider. I know because I did that for a living for a few years. Rangemen don't make in their lifetimes as much money as there is in your saddlebags."

Tennant looked up at the older man. "And so you think I stole it and that you are helping an outlaw?"

Jorge glanced over his shoulder again before replying. Antonia had been gone long enough to fill fifteen cups with wine. Maybe she was doing the supper dishes. Women! He faced forward and said, "I don't think anything. You can be whatever you are, amigo, and you don't have to tell me anything. But I want you to think about something. If they find you in my house and you are a renegade, Gringo law won't only put me in prison . . . You understand?"

Frank Tennant looked steadily at Jorge, then said, "I understand. I'm having trouble staying awake. Could we talk again tomorrow?"

Instead of replying, Jorge leaned, snugged the blanket up beneath the wounded man's chin, smiled, and left the room. Five minutes later Frank was asleep.

In the kitchen Antonia looked up as her father appeared in the doorless opening. She was drying her hands, the supper dishes were neatly stacked. He pulled out a chair and sat down as she said, "I was going to bring the wine now."

"Not now. He was very tired. I wanted the wine to keep him awake. But maybe it would only have made him sleepier."

She filled a cup for him and placed it on the table where he was sitting. "Did he say anything about the saddlebags?"

"No." Jorge sipped wine. "I don't know how a man gets that much money without stealing it. Maybe he robbed a bank or a train." He sipped again before continuing. "But— I guess it was from the look in his eyes, otherwise I can't explain it—but I am not sure he stole it."

Antonia would have refilled his cup, but he placed a calloused hand palm down over the cup. As she was turning away with the jug, his eyes followed her. It was good wine made from grapes of the bedraggled and unkempt vines that grew in the Mission yard. "We must do something with his horse—everyone knows we don't own a horse."

She came to the table and sat opposite him. "I can take it to Dominguez Canyon."

He raised his eyes to her face. He should have thought of that. Dominguez Canyon was about five or six miles northeast of the Mission. It was a deep, wide place where subsurface water provided nourishment for half a mile of flourishing undergrowth, trees, and grass. It was a favorite place for mustangs and other wild animals to browse, tank up, and leave.

People occasionally went out there seeking strayed goats or wandering milk cows, otherwise they avoided the place because not too long ago Indians had hidden there waiting to ambush people. There were still a few bands of holdouts, but no Indians had been in the vicinity of Guadalupe for years. "You should leave before sunrise," he said. "In the dark."

She nodded. "It's not just the horse, Father. What about the saddlebags?"

"I'll take care of them," he told her, arising from the table. "I'll hide them behind the stones in one of the monk cells at the Mission. No one ever goes to those little rooms, and even if they did, they wouldn't know which of the stones of the walls are not set in mortar. But I know. Good night, *dulce*."

She sat for a while, then mechanically took his cup to the washtub, and after scrubbing and drying it, hung it from one of the worn wooden pegs either his father or grandfather had embedded in the adobe wall near some shelves, which were for dishes and cooking pans.

Antonia Medina had a wide, serene forehead, eyes that were perfectly set in a round face with a hint of angularity, probably inherited from her father because her mother's face had been softly round. She had inherited other things from her father: his thoughtfulness and his prudence. And his toughness. She did not wait until near dawn to take the horse to Dominguez Canyon. She left the yard, riding bareback an hour or so after she knew her father would be asleep.

It was a warm night full of desert fragrance. There was a sickle moon and a rash of stars, but if there hadn't been she still would have known her way. The horse was recovering from hard use; he plodded along with dumb-brute obedience right up until he picked up the scent of wet earth and grass. After that he moved with more willingness.

She came to the verge from the northwest because there was no other suitable trail going down into the canyon. Here, the fragrance was a little stronger and the air was cooler, things Antonia noticed. But the horse was preoccupied with his impatience to get down where there was succulent green feed.

At the place where she slid to the ground and removed the bridle, there was grass past her ankles. The horse was anxious. She had to tug his head up twice before he'd remain still until the bridle was removed. Then he began eating as she stepped back to watch him briefly before heading back up the wide trail to the top-out. Up there she leaned to look at him again, but he had already gone through a thicket to a watery sump where he was hidden by trees.

She had no need to hurry back. It was barely midnight. With the bridle draped over one shoulder, she was busy with thoughts when a large rodent-hunting owl came within fifteen feet before it began to frantically beat the air with powerful wings for altitude. Owl flight is soundless unless something startles low-flying foragers, then as they try desperately for altitude, their wings make a loud whispery flutter.

Antonia stopped dead in her tracks with a beating heart until she saw the terrified bird. She laughed at him and started forward again.

Dogs barked as she approached Mex town. She ignored them, but as she was passing the large, darkly brooding old

Mission she became watchful—occasionally town dogs did more than bark. Generally they were harmless, but every town, particularly places like Mex town, had dogs that stalked anything they suspected might be approaching for trouble. She knew most of the Mex town dogs, including several with reputations for attacking people in the night.

Tonight though, there was only the barking. By the time she reached home the fragrance, as well as the warmth, were yielding to predawn cold. She guessed it would be perhaps five or six o'clock in the morning. She hid the bridle in the goat shed out back, went inside, and got ready for bed.

A quiet, masculine voice spoke in darkness from the direction of the parlor. "You are *coyote* for a woman, *dulce*. My way, no one would have seen you leave, but they might have seen you walking back. Your way, no one would see you coming or going. Good night."

"Why are you awake?" she asked, and got back a reply she would not have anticipated. "Because our visitor was having a nightmare and made cries."

"Is he all right now, Father?"

"Yes. You know, there is nothing to compare with a glass of wine to settle the mind. Good night."

"Good night—Father?"

"Yes, *dulce*?"

"I was thinking on the walk back . . ."

"Ah. Always a bad omen—women thinking."

She ignored that. "Frank won't be able to ride for a very long time."

"I know that. It is late and my legs are getting cold."

She ignored that too. "Every day he is here in the house with us increases the chance of something happening—someone finding out that we have him."

This time Jorge's reply was not entirely patient. "I know that. I've thought about it. There is only one answer, Antonia—you and I will say nothing. Neither will Frank—even if he could. And we will go on as we always have, trusting in

God and listening to the gossip and watching carefully. Good night!"

After he left she went to bed but did not sleep. Not entirely because her last remark to her father was bothering her, but also because after that five-mile walk, she was wide awake. In fact, she only had dozed off when the roosters of Mex town began lustily heralding the arrival of a new day.

Over in Gringo town, the early-morning mail stage went noisily northward out of town, its racket carrying bugle clear in all directions.

Antonia lay motionless for a long while and stirred finally when she heard her father stamping into his boots. Then she arose swiftly to start breakfast.

There were still roosters crowing.

CHAPTER 3

An Untypical Day at the Harness Works

BUD Shilling had already arrived at the shop as usual, got a fire lighted in the small cast-iron stove, and had put the coffeepot atop it when George Medina arrived. As he did every morning, Bud said, *"Buenos días,"* and George replied as he did every morning, in English. "Good morning."

Bud looped the strings of his apron while gazing at the back-leather rolled in damp gunnysacking on his worktable. "We got three rough-looking strangers in town," he said while approaching the table to unroll the damp leather. The trick was to have it pliable enough to work, but not wet.

Straddling the sewing horse, George worked on finishing a set of triple-leather harness tugs for the stage company across the road and northward. As he reached for his awl, he turned to look at his employer and said, "There are always strangers passing through."

Bud was aligning a tin pattern for pigeon-wing skirts atop the soft leather with his back to George. "Yeah, except that these three took Marshal Bierk to a table and sat talkin' with him for half an hour. Drinkin' and talkin'."

George considered the tug he had left clamped in the sewing horse last night. He remained expressionless, but inside he felt as if this was a bad premonition. "Did you talk to the marshal afterward?"

"No. He took them strangers across to his office." Shilling was bending over to carefully outline the tin pattern on the leather. "Manhunters, George. Sure as we're sittin' here."

George went to work with his awl and the four-twist, waxed

17

tan thread with its two needles. "We get them too," he murmured, and concentrated on his work. This time though, his hands were not as steady as they usually were.

The boss had either exhausted the topic or was too engrossed in cutting out the saddle skirts to say any more, but a half hour later, when he filled two cups and put one within reach of George and returned to the cutting table with the other cup, he said, "It's been my experience around here that when three manhunters ride in, it's not just some penny-ante horsethief they're after."

George sewed and said nothing.

"Most likely they're lookin' for a bankrobber, or maybe a murderer."

When George still said nothing, Bud sighed and went back to work. An hour later, one of the yardmen from the stage company's corralyard came over to see if the tugs were ready—they weren't. After he'd left, Bud mentioned again the affair of three hard-bitten strangers probably being manhunters. This did not, right at the moment, appear unusual to George. Then Bud said, "You know what criminal limitation is?" When George said he had no idea and did not believe he'd ever heard the term before, Bud explained.

"It's when a feller does somethin' and they don't catch him for maybe six or eight years. The law says if he isn't caught within about three years, why then he can't be prosecuted, can't even be hauled back where he done the crime."

George pushed through the left needle, pulled the thread snug, pushed the right needle through the same hole and had to pull harder to get it snug that time, then he leaned on the sewing horse's curved high jaws and turned to look at the back of his employer, but only briefly before returning to work. After a while he said, "It might be true, Bud, but I've seen the law arrest men wanted for killings long after they'd done it."

Shilling spoke without looking around. "That's different. For murder they never let up. I'm talkin' about maybe stage robbery and the like. Even blowin' a bank safe. But not killin'."

George kicked the rachetted lock loose to move the tug, clamped it, and went to work again. "Did they look like lawmen?" he asked, and was answered without either man looking away from his work.

"I didn't see no badges, but they was wearin' coats—they could be lawmen. They could be fellers huntin' someone down for the reward." Bud made a harsh little laugh. "They got fertile ground on the South Desert where every other son of a bitch is either hidin' out or hightailin' it for the border."

George finished with the second tug, put them flat out on a table, and beat the places where he had sewn them with a rawhide mallet until the thread was half buried in its grooves. An inflectionless, hard voice spoke from beyond the shop's counter. "Glad you got 'em finished. We need 'em."

Bud looked up at the weathered, unsmiling face of the rawboned, graying man who had spoken and smiled. "I told you yesterday it'd be a while, Sam."

George took both traces and put them flat out atop the counter before raising dark eyes to meet the slatey-gray gaze of the company's corralyard boss, Sam Smith. "Kept at it," George said. "You said it was a rush job."

Smith hoisted the traces, draped them from his shoulders, and nodded at Medina. He did not smile but he said, "You're a good man, George. Never let us down yet." He turned toward Bud. "How much?"

"Dollar. Four bits per tug."

Smith placed a silver cartwheel on the counter and walked out. Bud sighed as he went to the counter for the money. "Someday Sam's goin' to smile an' his face'll fall off."

George reached for the coal oil bottle, doused an old rag, and went to work methodically to get rid of the residue of beeswax on his hands. Bud went back to his table, and George took from a wall peg one of five old halters the liveryman had left about a week earlier to be repaired. The leather was stretched, bone dry, cracking, and dirty. It had never ceased to intrigue George that people whose living depended upon leather, rarely took care of it, and expected either Bud or George to make it like new in an hour or two, after they'd neglected it for several years.

He had to clean dried manure off the halter before lightly oiling it. Then he examined the length of the broken cheek-piece to be replaced and refilled his coffee cup before going to work.

There were two more interruptions. The first one was a grizzled old west-country cowman who had not been near a barber in months, and who hadn't changed his britches or shirt in about the same length of time. His name was Brent Campbell. He kept four riders, ran about eight hundred head, had a cow camp about twelve miles west of town. His herd grazed off the southern range until it dried up, then he trailed his cattle up north to better country where he owned thousands of good grassland acres.

He was rumored to be wealthy, but if appearance and taciturnity were evidence of being rich, he wasn't. As he leaned on the counter, shoved back his hat, and stripped off a pair of stained old gloves, he said, "How's it comin', Bud?"

Bud stepped away from his table and gestured. "It's comin', Mister Campbell."

"Still goin' to be a month, is it?"

Bud nodded while reaching for his cup. "Yeah, a month. This one won't wear out for fifty years."

Brent Campbell's little squinty eyes showed rough humor. "But I will, Bud. Still an' all, like I told you, nothin' but back-leather and the best of everything."

Bud nodded, swallowed coffee, and put the cup aside. "And seven-eighths double rigging. Mostly, I build 'em with full double rigging."

Campbell straightened up off the counter. "Yeah, I know, and mostly I guess it's all right. But over the past sixty years,

I've seen an awful lot of cinch sores on short-backed horses that if their riders would have had the sense of an idiot, they'd have known full double don't fit all horses but seven-eighths does. Well, I just come in with the wagon for supplies an' thought I'd look in."

Bud mechanically nodded. "Glad you did," he said, and watched the sinewy old man almost collide with Cord Bierk in the doorway. They nodded, Campbell walked southward, Marshal Bierk came up to the counter, eyed the pot on the stove, and said, "Is that fresh coffee, Bud?"

He filled a crockery mug and placed it in front of the big lawman. "Fresh as a man can make it," he said. "Just this mornin' I dropped in a new fistful of ground beans atop what was already in there."

Cord Bierk tasted the coffee and eyed Bud. "You make the best saddles I've ever seen, an' you turn out real fine harness, but I got to tell you, Bud, you're never in your misbegotten life goin' to make a decent cup of coffee."

George smiled and Bud did too. Cord considered the cut leather on the worktable. "Who's it for?"

"Brent Campbell, that feller you nearly run into at the door."

Bierk continued to eye the pieces of shaped leather. In the same conversational tone of voice, he said, "I been goin' up and down Main Street talkin' to the storekeepers." Bierk paused and brought his gaze back to Shilling. "I'm lookin' for a feller who raided a big ranch southwest of here, about fifty, sixty miles away. A hell of a hard ride from Guadalupe, down by Slaughterville. He made off with about thirty thousand dollars in greenbacks."

Bud's eyes widened. "Thirty thousand . . . from a damned cow outfit?"

Marshal Bierk ignored his friend's astonishment. "They run a lot of cattle. Thousands of them. They also got mining interests and run trade wagons down over the line into Chihuahua. Plumb down to Ciudad Camargo. It's a big company, Bud. They got a lot of drovers, riders, and whatnot workin' for 'em. It's sort of like a town or a fort. That thirty thousand was their workin' money."

"How did this feller get past all them hired hands an' get that money?"

Cord Bierk tried the coffee again and evidently found it less objectionable the second time because he half emptied the cup before answering. "All I know is that he got it an' some company men took after him, an' when that Santa Ana came, they lost him. They haven't been able to pick up his sign since. But they got close enough once to almost trap him. They think they shot him. He was ridin' a thoroughbred horse. He outran them, but last they saw before the wind stopped them, that feller was ridin' hunched over and holdin' to the saddle horn."

George Medina said, "Maybe he's dead. If they hit him bad, he didn't ride any fifty miles. He's lyin' out there somewhere."

Bud took it up. "Sure. Covered with dust, Cord."

Bierk nodded. "Yeah. That's what we talked about. Only those gents combed the area lookin' for him—and the horse. No sign anywhere."

George had a question. "Why did they come to Guadalupe?"

Bierk reached for the cup again but replied before raising it. "They been crisscrossing the country. Guadalupe is in the area where they figure he's got to be. Him or his remains." Bierk drained the cup before finishing what he had to say. "It's not him they're hunting so much. They don't even know who he is. It's his saddlebags they want. They told me last night in my office at the jailhouse that they don't like the notion of goin' back empty handed. Seems the *jefe máximo* of this ranch, a feller named Charles Burton, isn't the least bit interested in excuses or failures."

Marshal Bierk straightened up off the counter as Bud Shilling said, "All right. What's this feller look like?" Bierk did not seem to like the question. "Bud, I told you they don't know who he is. Some of the *arrieros* said they saw a stranger, a *norteamericano*, in the yard the afternoon of the day of the robbery. They described him as being sort of tall, sort of lean, dark skinned but not Mexican, wearin' a six-gun with ivory grips. The riders never got a close look at him, even when they wounded him."

Bud was going through trouser pockets beneath his old apron for a plug of tobacco, when he made a snorting sound. "Cord, you just described a hunnert strangers that've gone through town in the last month or two. Except for the gun."

Bierk glumly nodded his head. "Yeah, I know. That's what I told those gents who ride for Mister Burton. One of 'em said they'd been told that before."

George Medina had another question. "Are they going to leave town?"

"They already did," replied the lawman. "First thing this morning. They're goin' to backtrack and search every arroyo, every mound of wind-blown dirt. I'll tell you one thing—those three aren't goin' to quit until they've found those saddlebags with the money in 'em."

"Suppose someone else's already found his carcass and the saddlebags?" Bud asked, then gnawed at a corner of his molasses-cured plug.

Bierk looked pensive. "I wouldn't want to be in their boots," he replied. "If someone did that, they'd have done it after the Santa Ana. They'd sure as hell have left tracks. Those three gents look to me like men who could track a fly across a piece of glass."

George turned his back to the counter and went to work on the broken halter. A few moments later, after Cord Bierk had left the harness works to visit the next store on the east side of Main Street, Bud Shilling refilled his cup, and while gazing at the drying cut-outs on his table, quietly said, "You know something, George? This damned country's full of men who'll live out their years and die down here because they pulled off a robbery that didn't get them a third as much as thirty thousand dollars. I'll tell you what I know from experience—whoever that feller was, sure as hell he knew in advance how much money was in that safe or strongbox, and maybe was hid somewhere in the building where it was kept."

George turned his head slowly and gazed at Bud, but Bud was scowling at the table in front and did not notice the look he got. Nor did it occur to the boss that when he'd said he knew from experience how that robbery had been accomplished, he had confirmed what George Medina had suspected: that Bud Shilling was one of those individuals he had said would live out their years and die on the South Desert because they dared not return to wherever they had come from.

Bud ran a calloused hand over the cut-out seating-leather as he said, "Lord! Thirty thousand dollars!"

George began cutting away the broken ends of the halter's cheekpiece. *And a crucifix with a solid gold cross!*

CHAPTER 4

The Scent of Danger

ANTONIA listened to her father over a supper neither of them more than picked at. When he was finished, she said, "They can't find him, Father."

He shrugged.

"Frank needs a month."

He saw the fear in her lovely face and said, "I don't know these men, *dulce*. I didn't even see them. But they impressed the marshal, and that's good enough for me. Still, we'll do everything possible to see that Frank has his month. . . ." His voice trailed off. She watched his face in the shadows of candlelight. He caught her watching him and smiled. "Well, how is he today?"

"I didn't change the bandages. After what you said last night, I thought you would want to do that. Otherwise, he is eating much better. Tonight he was actually hungry. And he joked with me."

Her father arose. "You go change the bandages," he said, and at the stare he got, he also said, "I'm going to hide his saddlebags at the Mission. There didn't seem to be any hurry before today." He shrugged. "Maybe there is no hurry now either, but if I've learned one thing from life, it is not to put off what should be done. You look after him, and when I get back the three of us can talk."

"Should I tell him about the three men and what Marshal Bierk said at the shop?"

Her father stood a moment thinking, then nodded at her. "I'll be back as soon as possible," he said, and went after the saddlebags.

It was less than a half mile to the old Mission with its askew cross atop a bell tower from which the brass bells had been removed half a century ago to be melted down and made into cannon.

The resident priest was a fat, swarthy holy man known as Father Francis. He had done little to halt the decay of the old Mission, but he held services most of the day every Sunday and made regular rounds of Mex town, and less frequent visits in Gringo town.

The Medina men had served the Mission in varying capacities for a hundred years. Jorge had played there as a child, had worshipped there very faithfully most of his life, and had explored the big old building until he was as familiar with it as any of its caretaking priests had been. In fact, he was more familiar with it than its current priest was.

He knew how to avoid Father Francis, who knelt in solemn prayer after supper every night for an extended period of time.

In this instance there was no difficulty because the dingy, little-worn stairway of stone leading below the great covered stone walkway, which extended the full length of the church out back, was near the southern end of the loggia, whereas the shadowy great place of worship, with its ingrained scent of incense and its very old and very graphic carving of the crucified Christ behind the ornate high altar, was at the far upper end of the building.

As a child, Jorge Medina had taken six months to get up enough courage to descend those narrow stone stairs, which were always in darkness. Tonight he kept one hand on the rough wall until the stairs ended and a narrow walkway abruptly turned eastward. The darkness was deeper down here. He moved without hesitation—slowly, feeling both walls for the rotting narrow oaken doors of the monk cells. He counted three doors and halted at the fourth one, pushed his way inside, had to walk slightly bent, and put the saddlebags on the stone floor until he could strike a match whose fiercely sputtering bluish white brilliance was accompanied with a strong scent of sulphur.

He let the match die and approached the west wall, knelt and felt for the loose stone he had first discovered as a child in his early teens. There was a hollow place behind it, as though the original stonemason, long dead now, had deliberately provided this secret place. He pushed the saddlebags in, raised the large stone and fitted it back into place, then remained briefly, kneeling to make a short prayer before feeling his way back to the base of the stairs.

Above, someone was walking.

He waited, head slightly to one side. Whoever was up there was not wearing boots. It could be someone from Mex town wearing sandals; it could be Father Francis. Jorge was not worried about being discovered at the dark base of the stone stairway, he was worried about who was up there, what he was doing here at this time of night, and which way he would go.

The whispery sound of leather over stone diminished, then died out altogether. Jorge started up the stairs, one at a time. When he could raise his head and look both ways along the loggia, a pair of distant voices speaking in Spanish came back to him. Whoever was up there had met someone near the northern extent of the covered walkway. One voice he recognized instantly as Father Francis said, "Is it branded?" and the second voice, less deep and resonant, replied shortly. "Yes, Father, on the left shoulder, but I have never before seen this mark."

"What were you doing up there? Dominguez Canyon is not a safe place."

"I had to go, Father. I did not want to go and I took a pistol. My best milk goat . . . I tracked her by daylight."

"Was she up there?"

"Yes, Father. I was tying the rope around her neck when I heard the horse and went looking for him. He is a tall, very fine horse, Father. If I'd had another rope, I'd have led him back with my goat."

Father Francis's voice sounded firm as he said, "If it is a branded horse, my son, it belongs to someone. Probably one of the range cattlemen. If you had brought him back and put him in your pen, and someone saw him there, the marshal would come. You did right to leave him. Cattlemen who find one of their horses in a Mex town corral have been known to return in the night and hang people. Leave him. Forget you ever saw him."

"But Father, he is a fine animal, very valuable. With that kind of horse . . ."

"With that kind of horse, my son, you could get your neck broken. Leave him!"

"Yes, Father."

Jorge heard hurrying feet in flopping sandals hastening toward him and retreated to the bottom step where he waited for the better part of an hour after the man who had been to Dominguez Canyon had gone past. Then he climbed to the walkway and made certain Father Francis was no longer out there. Jorge went back the way he had come, entered the house, heard voices in the little back room where Frank Tennant was bedfast, and before going there filled a cup with wine and drank it like water.

The big thoroughbred bay horse! He had not risked peeking to see who the man was who had found it, and who had hurried past Jorge's hiding place, but of one thing he was sure because he knew the people of Mex town: the presence, as well as the hiding place of Frank Tennant's animal, would be told and retold throughout Mex town tomorrow, and the day after that it would reach Gringo town.

He put the empty cup aside and went toward the voices coming from the back of his house.

The basin Antonia had used while changing bandages showed only a very faint pinkness. She had put three candles in place, and their light combined with the light from the candle niche on the far side of Frank's bed brightened the room very well. Antonia and Frank looked up the moment her father appeared in the doorway. She said simply, "I told him."

Her father gazed at the man in the bed. His face was still sunken, bones showed prominently, but his beard was beginning to look less like stubble and more like something he had cultivated.

Jorge leaned in the doorway to speak, but Frank spoke first. "We've been arguing. I've got to get away from here."

Jorge's dark brows went up as he regarded the wounded man. "How? Someone found your horse in Dominguez Canyon. I don't know who he is, but I heard him telling the priest at the Mission that he had found this fine horse branded on the left shoulder. But even if you could dress yourself, you can't ride. You couldn't go a mile."

Frank's eyes met Medina's black stare. "If I don't leave, they're eventually going to find me in your house."

Antonia crossed her arms anxiously. "How? Father, that's what we've been arguing about. How could they find him here?"

From what Cord Bierk had said at the harness shop, the Burton ranch manhunters were going back over their trail; after that they intended to comb the countryside in all directions. The South Desert around Guadalupe was big. Jorge shifted position and spoke to Frank instead of Antonia. "I think you have a month," he told the younger man. Then he smiled. "I'll know the minute they come back to town. By then, if God is willing, you will at least be able to walk. Tell me—they are sure they hit you. How did they happen to hit you three times?"

Frank Tennant's explanation was cryptic. "I watched them from hiding, figured their course, and made a sashay toward a canyon intending to hide until they had gone past. They didn't go past—they headed for the canyon. I don't see how they could have known I was there. Anyway, I had to make a run for it. They started firing about the time I charged out of the canyon. I wasn't hit the first time until I was almost in the clear. That was the slug that gouged my lower left side. They ran their horses as fast as they could to stay in range. The next two shots hit me in the back but from a very great distance, otherwise they'd have killed me."

Jorge shook his head. "They knew they'd hit you. They think you may be dead somewhere on the range, maybe covered with dust and dirt from the Santa Ana. That's what they're doing now—looking for either your body or your horse."

Frank surprised both the Medinas when he said, "They're professional manhunters. They are brothers. Al, Pete, and Ash Duran, part Mex. That's what they do for Charles Burton—hunt down anyone on both sides of the border who tries to raid Burton's trade caravans. Or anyone he wants tracked down and killed."

Antonia was staring at Frank before he had finished speaking. "You know those men?"

He nodded. "Not well, but well enough to know who they are and what they do for Burton."

Jorge moved into the room, closer to the bed. "Do you know Charles Burton too?" he asked.

Frank shifted his attention from the girl to her father. "Yes, I know him. He is my uncle."

Again, the Medinas stared.

Frank tried to push up into a sitting position and would not have been able to do it if Antonia hadn't moved quickly to support him. He spoke to her father. "Did those men say anything about the money to Marshal Bierk?"

"All he said about that in the shop was that the money was Charles Burton's working capital."

Frank made a bitter smile. "I guess he could say that—that was my mother's money, what was left from her mother's estate after my grandmother died. She kept it in our ranch house near Albuquerque, in an oaken box under the floor. I was bringing cattle down from Colorado. When I got home, my mother had died when the house caught fire."

Jorge said, "Is that what really happened?"

Frank's answer was curt. "I thought so. It could have happened like that. But when I was clearing everything away after the funeral, there was no money under the floor."

"It could have burned," Medina said.

Frank shook his head. "It was gone before the fire. If the box had burned, the money would have burned too. What I found was the hardware from the box, the hasp and lock, the steel reinforcements for the corners of the box, but nothing in the charred oak that could have been money. The lock was broken before the fire."

"That's all?"

"No. A rangeman who worked on the adjoining ranch saw a band of men crossing the country in the late afternoon of the day of the fire. He recognized one of them. Charley Burton."

Antonia frowned. "In the late afternoon? The cowboy could have been mistaken. With poor light, if he was any distance away . . ."

"Antonia," Frank interrupted with anger. "He wasn't any distance away. He was south of the house when my uncle and his men rode in. He heard my uncle call to my mother to come out and bring the money with her. They didn't see him—he hid in an arroyo until the house was afire and my uncle was riding away."

Jorge looked aghast. "His own sister?"

"That wouldn't bother him. Both my father, when he was alive, and my mother knew what her brother was. I heard them say so several times when they didn't know I was in the house. I went after the money. There was something else—a rosary with a large gold crucifix my father gave my mother the summer they were married. It was in the sack with the money when I found them. It didn't melt when the house burned because it was not in the house during the fire and neither was the money."

Antonia allowed Frank to ease gently back down in the bed. She put both hands over her face and ran from the room. Her father pulled the little stool close and sank down upon it. "How did you know where to find the money?" he asked.

"I worked cattle for my uncle two years before he killed my mother and stole her money. I knew his house and office as well as I know my own house, the one he burned. I quit him to buy cattle in Colorado and drive them south to sell around the Albuquerque country. Mister Medina, I didn't just go after the money, I went after my uncle. He was down in Mexico, so he is still alive. But I'm going back."

Jorge sat hunched on the little stool staring at the sweaty, twisted face of the younger man. "It won't be for a very long time, Frank. It may never be. He can't be a fool, so he will know who took the money from him. He will know you will hunt him down someday. How many men like the Duran brothers work for him?"

Frank wasn't sure but he made a guess. "About ten like those and about fifty others."

Jorge arose. "Go to sleep. You don't look very well. Would you like some wine?"

"No thanks."

"Go to sleep."

"I don't think I can."

"Try. Don't think about those other things. Sleep, rest, eat as much as you can."

Frank rolled his eyes upward toward the older man's face. "And pray?"

Jorge stood a moment gazing downward, then turned without answering and went to the kitchen where Antonia was sitting staring into the light of a candle. As he dropped down he said, "He asked me if he should pray." Jorge looked bleakly at his daughter across the table.

She said, "You told him to?"

"No! A man has no right to pray for God's help to kill another man, no matter how bad the other man is."

"Father, would you like a cup of wine?"

He smiled across the table. "Very much. It is late. Then we must go to bed."

CHAPTER 5

Marshal Bierk's Hunches

SPRINGTIME on the South Desert brought not only flowers and bunchgrass, it also brought freighters, increased loads of passengers and mailbags on stagecoaches, and every imaginable kind of drummer, from those peddling weapons and hardware, to the ones with samples of bolt goods, the latest styles from Paris, and overpoweringly fragrant toilet water.

There was an ordinance against freight outfits using Main Street. They were required to pass by town either on the east or west side beyond the alleyways and the nearest habitations. There were occasional exceptions, but not many.

Old Brent Campbell occasionally arrived in town with his unshorn, faded, beard-stubbled and sun-bronzed riders. Brent and Will Perkins at the saloon had been friends for more than ten years.

Brent was nursing a five-cent beer at Perkins's bar with his six battered and hard-looking riders strung out southward, also with glasses of beer, when Campbell said, "You know, Will, I been comin' down here for the springtime grass for about forty years. In that time they've had about two dozen town marshals and six or seven saddle makers. But if you want to see an example of the best saddle maker this place ever had, go out front an' look at that new saddle in my ranch wagon. I tell you, Bud Shilling's got talent that won't quit."

Will did not go look at the new saddle; he refilled his old friend's glass and smiled. "I know. Just about everyone in town's been watchin' that rig come together. How long did it take 'im?"

"About three months, but that didn't matter. What I

wanted was the absolute best in everything. This here will be the last saddle I ever ride. I was in about a month and a half ago when him an' George Medina was talkin' about some strangers that'd just rode into town. He was beginning to shape the under-seat at that time. I figured it'd be another couple months. No sir, by gawd. I went in this morning to see how he was comin' and so help me Hannah, there it sat, finished and as handsome as anything you ever saw."

Marshal Bierk came by to see Brent Campbell. He'd seen the cowman leave Bud's shop heading for the saloon with his riders. As Will set up a beer for the lawman, Cord inquired about cattle prices, losses due to rattlesnakes, red-water and the other things that killed cattle, and he also mentioned the weather, which was an almost indispensible preliminary in any conversation with stockmen. Old Brent went through the ritual patiently, and when the opening arrived he said, "What's on your mind, Marshal?"

Cord downed half his beer before settling comfortably against the bar and saying, "I got a big thoroughbred-lookin' bay horse impounded down at the public corrals I'd like you to look at."

Campbell nodded. "All right. Is it a stray?"

"Seems to be. A feller who owns goats over in Mex town found him up at Dominguez Canyon. I rode out and brought him back. Fine animal, Brent. In his prime, no gall marks."

"When'd you bring him in?"

"About ten days ago."

"Branded?"

"Yes. On the left shoulder. But it's not a local mark. I thought you bein' from up north, you might know the brand."

Campbell shoved away his empty glass and turned. "Let's go see him," he said, and led the way to the roadway, then southward in the direction of the public corrals, which adjoined the private corrals, and the combination wagon works and livery barn belonging to a man named Kent Duncan, who hadn't seen his belt in years because of a big gut.

Kent was a graying man with little, shrewd eyes. He had arrived in Guadalupe seven years earlier with a ridden-down horse, two guns, and both pants pockets stuffed with greenbacks. Since then he had prospered, had grown soft and fat, and had also gotten into the wagon sales and repair business.

He was leaning on the outside stringers of the public corrals when Campbell and Bierk arrived. He turned aside to expectorate before nodding, then jutted his jaw in the direction of the fleshed-out, handsome bay horse inside the corral. "Valuable animal," he opined. Brent Campbell, who was a short man, stepped onto the lowest stringer to have a clear view of the horse. He did not say a word for a long time, then he climbed back down and addressed Marshal Bierk. "Don't know the mark, Cord, but I'll tell you what I'll do. You let me know the day you're goin' to put him up for sale for the impound, and I'll make it a point to be here to bid on him."

Kent Duncan turned aside again to spray amber, then turned back. "I sort of had in mind bidding on him, Mister Campbell."

Brent said, "It's a free country," nodded, and walked away. For a while Kent was silent as he studied the bay horse, then he told Marshal Bierk since he'd been pitching feed to the bay horse and sort of looking after him, he figured he'd ought to have the last bid when the animal went up for auction.

Bierk did not commit himself. "It'll be a while. I got some letters out about that brand. I won't put him up for sale until I get some answers. Sure as hell someone ought to know something about that horse."

Kent shifted his stance, hitched at his britches, and nodded. "If he belonged to me, you can bet your wages I'd be lookin' for 'im."

Cord smiled a little. "Yeah. That's what I'm hopin' might happen one of these days."

Kent faced the lawman with a faint frown. "You got some idea about this horse?"

"Not an idea, Kent. More like a pretty poor hunch." Cord Bierk walked away, leaving the liveryman gazing after him with a baffled expression.

When the marshal returned to his jailhouse office, Brent Campbell was sitting there, feet shoved out, old hat tipped back, fully relaxed and drowsy. He pushed up straighter in the chair when Bierk walked in.

Cord was surprised but tried not to show it as he went to his old table and sat down. "Something about the bay horse?" he asked.

The old cowman's habitually narrowed eyes went from the gunrack on the west wall to the big man behind the table. "No. No connection. It's about some fellers me'n my boys been runnin' into now an' then the past month or so. Three of 'em. First they're on the south range, then they're over west a ways, then the last time—a week or so back—they'd been campin' at one of our waterholes, an' that's the only time we come right up onto 'em. It was real early, before dawn. Otherwise, when they've seen any of us, they rode off in the opposite direction."

Cord let go a soundless sigh and leaned with both arms atop the table. "Did you talk to them?"

"Yep. They was fixin' to break camp when we come up. We knew they was there, so this time we sort of come in all around the spring. If they'd been on horseback they might've made a run for it. They wasn't. They was on foot."

"What did they say?"

"That they was lookin' for someone."

"What else?"

"Damned little," Campbell replied dryly. "I've seen a hunnert just like 'em in my time, Cord. Manhunters."

"Mexicans?"

"Well, maybe half. The oldest-lookin' one was called Ash by the other two. We heard 'em call him that as we rode up onto 'em, but when I asked their names they said Smith, Jones, an' Johnson." Campbell leaned forward a little in his chair. "They sort of annoyed me, so I told 'em campin' at one of our springs kept the cattle from drinkin' there. I told 'em we run close to a thousand head down here and don't take kindly to strangers gallivantin' around, makin' the cattle uneasy, an' if I come onto 'em again I was goin' to make certain they got the hell off our range and stayed off it."

Marshal Bierk studied Campbell's face. He and Brent had always gotten along very well, but he had heard many stories about the old cowman's temper. "What did they say about that?" he asked.

"Nothing. Not a damned word. Two went after their horses while one stayed at the camp to finish up. We rode away. But I been thinkin' about that for a week. It's one of the reasons I came to town today. To let you know if I have any more trouble with those men, they're goin' to wish they'd listened to me." As Brent Campbell arose from the chair, he put a quizzical gaze upon Marshal Bierk. "Seems to me, Cord, other folks must have seen those three. Have you heard about 'em before I come in here?".

Bierk studied his clasped hands for a long moment before saying, "Sit down, Brent."

The cowman sat down.

"Their name is Duran."

"All three of 'em?"

"Yeah. They're brothers and work for a man named Charles Burton. Someone robbed Burton of thirty thousand dollars and rode in this direction. The Durans are looking for him, but mostly to get the money back."

For fifteen minutes Campbell and Marshal Bierk talked, then the old cowman reset his hat and left the jailhouse looking incredulous. His final words to the lawman had been: "All right, I'll believe it all except the part about thirty thousand dollars. You got any idea how much money that is? A man could buy this whole blessed town and all the decent grazing country around it for that kind of money. Maybe those fellers meant thirteen thousand dollars, or maybe they said thirteen and you didn't hear right."

Cord Bierk continued to sit at his desk long after Campbell's departure. Maybe he hadn't heard right. Maybe the Durans had said thirteen thousand dollars, which was still more money than he would ever see in one pile if he lived to be two hundred. But he knew what he had heard; the figure had been repeated a number of times.

He arose and strolled up the west side of Main Street, crossed over, and encountered fat Kent Duncan emerging from Bud's leather shop with a number of repaired halters slung over one shoulder. When they met, Kent said, "You see these damned halters? Well sir, I left them to be repaired a month ago an' they just now finished 'em."

Bierk's policy was to be neutral in situations of this kind, so he said, "Looks like they did a good job though," and watched the paunchy liveryman cross diagonally toward the opposite plankwalk, then entered the saddle and harness works, which had an aroma more pleasing to most men than the smell down at Will Perkins's saloon.

Bud was working on a set of old chain harness. Someone had crudely sewn heavy canvas around each chain-trace to prevent a horse's legs from being chafed and bruised. Whoever had done that had undoubtedly been motivated by humane consideration, but Bud had been swearing all morning as he tried to cut through the thread and canvas to remove the coverings, so his disposition was not its best when Marshal Bierk sauntered in and leaned on the counter.

George Medina was working on a saddle seat a horse had torn loose in a pitching and kicking fit. He smiled at the lawman. "How's the law business?" he asked. "The leather business has been good lately."

Bud finally glanced up from his work, shaking his head. "I

should have listened to my paw. He was a baker, always worked in a clean store, made good wages, and didn't have to sweat over the damnfool things people do with leather."

Bierk eyed the worn old harness. "Years back I kept company with a girl whose paw had a sausage works. I had to give her up. At least this harness smells of leather and horses. That girl always smelled of garlic."

George laughed.

Bud made a weak smile as the marshal asked, "Has there been anyone come in to have a bridle or saddle worked on by the name of Duran?"

George's hand stopped moving. He did not look around in the direction of the marshal, but Bud scowled and slowly shook his head. Then he faced around. "George, you remember anyone by that name?"

He answered without turning. "No. How long ago, Marshal?"

"Well, Brent Campbell ran into them—there's three of 'em, brothers. He ran into 'em at one of his waterholes last week. But they've been around the country for almost two months. I believe I told you then that they're lookin' for a feller who robbed the man they work for down along the southwest border, made off with thirty thousand dollars. Anyway, I was curious if they've been in to have work done."

"No," George said. "Not that I know of. What about the man they're looking for?"

"George, I got no idea. But a few days back I impounded a bay horse some Mex goatherder found down in Dominguez Canyon."

George turned slowly. "Was it the horse of the man who took the money?"

"I can't answer that either," stated the lawman. "But I sent out some letters to see if I can find someone who knows the brand. If I get lucky an' someone writes back that they know the mark, why then it shouldn't be too hard finding out who owned the horse. It could be the same feller those Durans are lookin' for. If it is, then he didn't die out there during the Santa Ana."

Bud Shilling had been listening with interest. "If he rode the horse this far, then he's maybe somewhere close by. Is that possible, Cord?"

Bierk nodded his head. "Yeah, and if he is I want to get him before the Durans find him. He was shot up. The Durans darn near cornered him in a canyon and are sure they hit him as he was runnin' for it."

Bud settled against his worktable and crossed both arms across his chest. "Hell, Cord. If he was shot up and he's still alive somewhere close by, that'd mean someone took him in and doctored him."

Bierk gazed at the harness maker. "A man with thirty thousand dollars in greenbacks wouldn't have much trouble findin' someone who'd run the risk of keepin' him, tryin' to get him back on his feet."

George put down his leather tools and faced around. "Who, Marshal?"

Bierk regarded the older man thoughtfully for a moment before replying. "I don't know. But while I wait for an answer to them letters about the horse, I'm goin' to start nosin' around. George? I could sure use some help. Folks in Mex town forget all the English they ever knew and have lapses of memory when I just go down there for a *cerveza*."

George gently shook his head while looking steadily at the big lawman. "I couldn't do that."

Bierk did not push the issue, but as he was turning to leave he said, "Nobody's mentioned a reward, but I'd guess that Burton feller who lost all that money would be willin' to pay a decent amount to find his man an' get his money back."

CHAPTER 6

Villalobos

BUD Shilling followed Marshal Cord Bierk outside. "I could have told you George wouldn't do anythin' like that. But there's plenty of folks in Mex town who would."

Cord was watching a stagecoach coming up Main Street from the south. It made a wide sashay in order not to strike wheel-hubs on the big old scarred gateposts before it entered the corralyard. He sounded indifferent as he replied to Bud Shilling. "Yeah, the feller who found the big bay horse out at Dominguez Canyon."

Bud watched the lawman strike out in the direction of the corralyard, returned thoughtfully to the shop, and approached the stove to shake the coffeepot. It was empty. He set it aside, sighed, and went back to his worktable as he said, "Always something . . . George?"

"What?"

"That'd be a long time for manhunters to be pokin' around in one place, wouldn't you say?"

George was bending over the saddle with the torn seating-leather. "Seems that way."

"If they're professionals they wouldn't do it unless they had some notion the feller they want is close by."

"Yes . . . Bud, you left the lid off the gluepot again. It's like rubber."

"Boil some water. That'll soften it. You suppose anyone could be hidin' that outlaw down in Mex town?"

George was filling a small pan with water from their drinking bucket when he answered. "I think in Gringo town they'd be more likely to break the law for money."

Bud said no more, and George eventually got the glue

43

softened enough to apply it to the underside of the new seating-leather. He put small sandbags on the saddle seat and went back to refill their drinking-water bucket. Out there he stood a long time in solemn thought before returning. During his absence the corralyard boss, Sam Smith, the gruff, hard-eyed, unsmiling man, had brought over a set of light driving harness to be cleaned, oiled, and repaired. It was one of those California outfits that relied on a thick breast strap rather than a collar pad, a collar, and hames. Sam was growling to Bud Shilling about that kind of harness and barely glanced over at George as he put the bucket down and nodded.

"Never used to see harness like that," Smith was dourly saying. "Now it pops up all over the place, an' it's not worth a damn. A horse don't pull with his chest, he pulls with his legs and shoulders."

Neither Bud nor George argued—neither of them had any feeling one way or the other about California harness. Also, Sam Smith's disposition was well known around Guadalupe. He was a quick-tempered man with fists like stone.

After Smith departed, Bud turned and grinned. George grinned back. Not a word passed between them as they returned to their work.

With the sun on its way toward some hazy, distant mountains, Bud hung up his apron, waited until George had put aside his tools, then dug out two chipped old white cups and a bottle of red wine, and said, "I was thinkin', George. If someone'd stole that much money off me, I'd have a whole darned army of manhunters lookin' under every rock and inside every house." He held out one of the cups to Medina. "And somethin' else crossed my mind, George. It don't seem right that anyone should have that much money."

George repeated what old Brent Campbell had said to Bud Shilling down at the public corrals. "It's a free country."

Bud changed the subject after sipping his wine. "Tomorrow's Saturday. You want to come in?"

George finished the wine and leaned to put the cup aside as he replied. "It's also springtime. I work up the ground for my garden every spring. There's nothing that can't wait until Monday, is there?"

Bud also finished his wine. "Naw. Don't throw your back out diggin'. See you Monday."

Antonia was sweeping the hardpan in front of the house when her father came along. She watched him approach, put aside the broom, and entered the house to reach into the cooler for the burlap-wrapped jug. As he came to the kitchen doorway, she was setting up a cup for him at the table. He shook his head. "No thanks. Bud and I had a drink at quitting time." He leaned on the table, looking straight at his daughter. "Is he still braiding those reins?"

"No. He finished them. They are a present for you. He said something today . . . He wants to pay us for hiding him and taking care of him until he could walk."

Jorge Medina sat down. "Ask him to come in here. I have something to tell both of you."

While Antonia went after Frank, Jorge changed his mind and poured the cup half full. When Antonia returned with Frank, her father eyed the younger man, whose wounds had healed very well, and whose strength had gradually returned until now he stood there looking as strong, alert, and healthy as Jorge imagined he had probably ever looked.

Medina told them about the horse, about Bierk sending out letters about the horse's mark, and also about the Durans and Brent Campbell. When he finished, he drained the cup and shoved it away. Antonia sank down at the table across from her father, eyes large and hands locked together.

Frank Tennant did not sit down. He'd been restless for the last couple of weeks, like a caged wolf. Antonia had been afraid he would go outside in broad daylight, but he hadn't. Instead she brought him strips of rawhide, and he showed her how to plait and braid. But as Medina considered the younger man now, he mentioned Marshal Bierk's attempt to recruit him to look for someone in Mex town who could be hiding a fugitive.

Frank was pulled down to the bench by Antonia. He refilled her father's cup and drank half the contents before handing the cup to the older man. "I'm ready," he said. "I been ready for a week or two. Tell me something, Jorge. Could I go up to the corralyard and buy passage out of the country on the early-morning stage? Does the marshal know what I look like?"

Medina could only shrug. He could not recall Cord ever describing Frank Tennant, but perhaps he had—Medina's memory was not as good as it once had been. However, even if Cord had a description, he never circulated through town until well after sunup, and the early-morning stage left in the chilly dark of predawn.

And there was the silky chestnut beard that Frank had grown; he looked quite different from the way he had when they'd found him two months back. Medina nodded. "I think you could. It would be dark. No one is around but the corralyard men. Even the owner doesn't get out of bed to see the early-morning stage off."

Frank spoke crisply. "All right. In the morning. I hate to leave my horse behind. Did you say they're goin' to auction him off for the impound?"

"Yes."

"Jorge, if I leave you enough money will you bid him in?"

Medina spread work-calloused hands atop the old table. "Why would I need a horse? We haven't had a horse since I was a child."

"What's that got to do with it?"

Medina was gazing at the backs of his hands when he answered. "It would cause talk. You don't know how it is in Mex town. If anyone does something unusual, the gossip starts, then comes the speculation, and finally there are the fertile imaginations. Do you know what they'll be saying? That old Medina bought that outlaw's horse. From there it will be only one step until they say, of course he did, old Medina is the one who hid that outlaw until he was able to travel. Old Medina must have been paid a lot of money to do that."

Frank turned toward Antonia, wearing a skeptical expression. She nodded at him. "That is exactly what will happen, Frank."

He took down a big breath and sighed. "But that horse saved my life by being able to outrun the Durans. Before that we went a lot of places together. He never lost his head nor showed a fault."

Medina raised his shoulders and lowered them. He turned the discussion back to Frank's departure. "Never mind. I'll know who buys your horse and see that he isn't abused. As soon as it's dark I'll go get your saddlebags. Antonia can help you roll your things together. Now, I'm hungry, daughter. By now you must know wine makes men hungry."

She arose unsmilingly as she said, "So does talking." She approached the stove with her father's eyes following. Only lately had she made little sharp remarks like that. Every time he brought up the subject of Frank leaving, she got short with him.

Medina left his old hat behind and went out into the settling night. It was warm, there was a veritable rash of stars, springtime desert fragrance subtly filled the night air.

A wispy-thin, sharp-featured, very dark man appeared soundlessly out of nowhere, grinning from ear to ear. In Spanish he said it was a beautiful night, and Medina looked down his nose at the shorter man, whom he knew. His name was Cruz Villalobos. He grazed two dozen goats on the desert, owned two burros, was known throughout Mex town as a sneaky, sly, scheming individual, and was not well liked.

Medina agreed that it was a fine night and wondered aloud why Villalobos was out so late in the darkness. The answer he got settled a question that had not occurred to him. But perhaps it should have.

Cruz Villalobos edged close and almost whispered his reply. "You've heard about the fine bay that was found in Dominguez Canyon—well, I am the one who found him."

Medina gestured with his hands. "Does that tell me why you are out tonight? Oh—you expect to find another horse?"

"No, no, companion," Villalobos replied. He leaned even closer and finally did in fact whisper, "Marshal Bierk hired me. He thinks that horse belonged to an outlaw everyone is talking about in Gringo town, a man who stole thirty thousand dollars. He hired me to see if someone in Mex town is hiding this renegade. Over in Gringo town the marshal is doing the same thing. Between us, he says we might find this rider of other people's horses."

"I thought I heard you say he stole money, not horses."

Villalobos smirked. "Money, yes. I had no idea there was so much money on earth, did you, companion—thirty thousand dollars?"

Medina solemnly agreed, lightly tapped the smaller man on the shoulder, and turned to reenter his house. "Good hunting," he said.

Antonia and Frank were standing in darkness just beyond the door as her father walked in. He raised his eyebrows and Frank said, "We heard. She translated for me. Jorge, will Marshal Bierk sleep in tomorrow morning or will he be looking for me?"

Although he knew for a fact that the lawman normally did not appear until after daybreak, he could not be certain that tomorrow would not be the exception, so he shrugged. "I don't think so. What I *do* think is that the trap is ready to spring. Everyone knows about you by now. If we wait another few days or longer, I think your chances of escaping will be much worse."

Frank nodded in agreement, and the three of them returned to the kitchen. Medina sighed as he sat down. He had anticipated only having to exert normal caution in retrieving the saddlebags. Now, he was worried. Cruz Villalobos was *coyote,* naturally sly and sneaky. Now, having been hired to ferret out what he could in Mex town, Villalobos would be even more *coyote.*

He told his daughter and Frank to retire, that he would wait until midnight, then go after the saddlebags. Antonia seemed willing until Frank said, "I'll go with you. Two sets of eyes are better than one."

Medina went after the wine jug, filled a cup, and returned to the table with it. He smiled at them. *"En el país de los ciegos, el tuerto es rey,"* he said and sat down.

Antonia faced Frank. "It is an old saying. It means that in the land of the blind, the one-eyed is king. In other words, no one knows where you are. Only my father and I know."

Medina raised his cup. "Go to bed, Antonia."

She studied her father's face before arising, brushing one hand across Frank Tennant's shoulders on her way around the table to kiss her father, then she left.

Medina sipped his wine, eyed the younger man, and finally said, "Where will you go?"

"North. That's where I came from. The house is gone, but the barn and outbuildings are still there—or were when I saw them last. The land is good. We owned many sections, Jorge."

"He will send men there to find you, Frank. If they don't find you here, he'll send men to hide in a camp up there and shoot you in the back." Medina drained the cup. "Where have you never been? South toward Mexico, or maybe eastward? Go in one of those directions. But one day come back."

Frank smiled at the old man. It was getting late. Soon they should go after the saddlebags. "Yeah, someday, Jorge. I'll miss you too. You've been one hell of a friend."

Medina pushed up to his feet. "Not for me, friend. For Antonia." He turned away so he would not have to look at the younger man's expression, and said, "Go get your gun and meet me outside."

CHAPTER 7

Darkest Before Dawn

A COUPLE of dogs were barking, which would have had significance to an Indian. Medina led off westward into the darkness beyond his corral and shed, got those things behind them both before turning in the direction of the Mission. He halted several times to listen. Those two dogs were still barking. He shrugged; dogs always barked. Especially after nightfall. They did not have to have a reason, just an alien scent. Maybe a badger or a skunk foraging the garbage dumps of Mex town. Maybe they were barking at each other.

He turned. Frank also was listening to the night. He smiled slightly. They continued in a roundabout route until they were approaching the Mission from the north, the opposite direction from which Medina had approached before. On their right, pale knee-high stones, mostly with rounded tops, some leaning, some upright, were arranged in more or less straight rows. Medina brushed Frank's arm and gestured toward a particular stone. "My father," he said, and gazed at an adjoining pair of stones. "My mother and grandfather."

Ahead was the long loggia with its broad overhanging roof. Medina leaned to remove his boots. Frank took his cue from the older man and did the same. Soundlessly, they passed a faintly lighted room on their right where the parish priest lived, and continued down almost the full length of the concourse until Medina halted and, twisting from the waist, looked in all directions before approaching what appeared to Frank as a dark hole in the lower wall. As Medina descended, Tennant used his hands to feel his way. It was dark all the way to the bottom of the stone stairway and even darker below it. He moved up close in order to watch his guide. Medina felt along the west wall for a short distance, then turned right. Frank did the same.

The little cell of a room they entered smelled of stale air and mold. The older man approached a wall and knelt. Frank had to lean close to see what Medina was doing. As the big stone was lifted from its setting in the wall, Medina looked up and smiled. The saddlebags were still there. He pulled them out, handed them to Frank, and replaced the stone, then they returned to the loggia where it was not as dark and where the air was sweeter.

Medina said nothing as he now led off in a direct route for the house. He did not stop to listen and only occasionally turned his head. The dogs were no longer barking; the night was silent until something made a rustling sound over among the gravestones, which Medina ignored. Beyond the overhanging roof, starlight helped visibility but not very much. They took none of the precautions they had taken earlier.

When they arrived at the house, they saw that Antonia had left the jug and two cups on the kitchen table before retiring. She had also left a small lighted candle in one of the niches. Its light was only slightly better than the stars had been.

Frank dumped his saddlebags atop the table and sat down to unbuckle one and reach inside. He extracted a packet of greenbacks bound with a green ribbon.

Medina looked up from filling their cups. He said nothing but he had never seen money tied with a green ribbon before.

The young man pulled loose three bills and left them atop the table, then returned the packet to the saddlebags and buckled them.

As Medina sat opposite him, Frank shoved the money toward him. Medina shook his head, raised his cup, and smiled. "There are things people don't do for payment, friend." He hoisted his cup. "To the dawn stage leaving on time."

They drank, and Frank left the money on the table as he

arose. "I've got a couple of things to do before I bed down. What time in the morning, Jorge?"

"I'll waken you."

"Good night. I'm very grateful. Tell Antonia for me, will you?"

"Yes. Take your money."

Frank leaned, roughly cuffed the older man on the shoulder, grinned, and left the kitchen. Medina eyed the money. It was a small fortune. He scratched inside his shirt, left their cups and the jug on the table, took the money, and went to his room to sleep. Tomorrow was going to be one of those cliff-hanger days. He hadn't experienced one in almost thirty years. Since the death of his wife, he had lived a life of routine circumspection. Before dozing he grunted to himself. His life still would have been quietly routine if Frank Tennant had stumbled into someone else's goat corral.

Outside, the world was empty, silent, magnificently mysterious, and still faintly fragrant. Then it began to turn chilly.

Medina opened his eyes in darkness as someone gently shook him. His daughter, fully dressed and with her hair as shiny as obsidian in the dimness, said, "I have breakfast ready. Frank is dressing." As her father pushed up in the bed, she handed him a small packet. "I'm not going over to Gringo town with you. Before you leave him, give him this for me."

Medina hefted the little packet. It was very light and tied with a wrapping of scarlet yarn. He did not ask what it was; he simply shooed her out of his room so he could swing to the edge of the bed and reach for his shirt and britches.

When he entered the kitchen, Frank was already eating, and Antonia brought another platter and hot coffee for her father. Then she paused briefly behind Frank, put both hands on his shoulders, and spoke in Spanish. "May God protect you. Good-bye, Frank."

She left the room without even looking back. Tennant paused with a forkful of meat halfway to his mouth and turned, but she was gone, and her father cleared his throat. "Finish, *vaquero*."

Medina did not speak again until they had passed up through the west side of Mex town to the dogtrot he had used every morning for years. When they emerged upon the wooden plankwalk in Gringo town, Medina halted, handed Frank the little packet, said it was from his daughter, then smiled. "You will return someday."

Frank was studying the small packet as he replied. "Yes. When I can."

"Well, since we still have your saddle and bridle, it may not be too long."

Frank shifted the saddlebags on his shoulder and held forth the little packet. "What is this?"

Medina shrugged. "*Quién sabe?* Antonia gave it to me to give to you as we parted." Medina held up a hand. A pair of old lanterns had just come to life over in the corralyard. "You can pay for your passage to the yardman. His name is Sam Smith. I think he has been an outlaw of some kind. He is a man who never smiles. Frank . . ."

They shook hands, each with a tight grip. Frank wrapped one arm around the old man's shoulder and said, "I'll never be able to thank you enough. Will you tell Antonia for me that——?"

Medina nodded gently. "I will tell her. Listen. They are throwing on the harness, you'd better get over there. Adios."

Frank looked back twice as he walked down the wide roadway. The second time there was no sign of Medina.

There were two old smoking lanterns suspended from steel hooks bolted to a pole. If their wicks had been trimmed occasionally and their glass mantles had been cleaned, they would have lighted the entire yard. As it was, they shed light only as far as the faded and rugged stagecoach. One man was holding up the tongue of the coach while another man backed the wheel horses into place before the leaders were brought up and also put on the pole.

The third man with the coach was hatless and unkempt. His hair was dark, with silvery highlights, and looked as if it had not been combed recently. Although it was very early and there was no one around except Frank and the yardmen making the hitch, the hatless man wore a shellbelt and a holstered six-gun.

Frank remembered Medina's casual comment about someone called Sam Smith and approached as he said, "Good morning. I was told that if your name is Smith, I can pay you for a seat on the coach."

The man turned without changing the rhythm of his jaws, looked Frank up and down, turned to expectorate and said, "How far you goin'?"

"North. As far as the coach goes."

Sam Smith held out a hand. "Dollar an' you'll end up in a place called Pinole." As Smith pocketed the money, he spat again, then looked at Frank and wagged his head. Smith walked over to where one of the leaders had a leg over a trace. Without a word he lifted the leg, pulled the trace clear, and put the leg down.

One of the yardmen returned from the office with two wooden crates, which he put inside the coach, and went back for two more. When they had been loaded, the man smiled at Frank and said, "I left room for you."

They were turning the coach by hand so that the horses faced the big front gate, when Sam Smith sauntered over to Frank and said, "Strange thing. I'm here from before dawn until after dark every damned day but Sunday, an' I don't recollect seein' you come in on any of our stages."

Frank's answer was short. "I didn't get here by stage. I got here by horseback."

Smith accepted that. "All right. Your horse die?"

"No. I'll be back for him."

The coach was ready for boarding, so Frank nodded to the corralyard boss, went over to open a door to pitch his saddlebags in first, then climbed in. At the same time the driver went up the near side from the ground to a wheel-hub, and from there to a steel stirrup that gave him access to the boot and high seat. The driver did not accept the lines from a yardman until he'd cinched his coat up to the gullet, pulled on his elegant gauntlets, and placed his curled whip with the sterling silver ferrules up its handle into the whip socket. Then he leaned, accepted the lines, looked on both sides, kicked off the binders, talked up the hitch, and as the rig moved ahead he called down to the corralyard boss, "See you next week."

Smith nodded, raised his hand in an indifferent salute, and said nothing.

Dawn chill came into the coach from both sides. There were rolled-up blinds, but Frank made no move to lower them. The chill would last only another hour or so. Besides, he had never felt comfortable riding in a coach when he could not see out.

They were about two miles north when the whip's profanity was carried downward and rearward as the coach hauled down to a gradual halt.

When it stopped completely and the driver was scrambling down to the ground, Frank got out to see what had happened. The whip was a leathery-faced man with pale eyes, a big droopy mustache shot full of gray, and thick hands, which emerged from his gauntlets as he looked at Frank in monumental disgust. "Look. Did you ever see anyone in their right mind hook horses up with the traces uneven?"

Frank strode up where the whip was pointing. He shook his head. "Nope, I never did. It was too early for those yardmen to have been drinking."

The driver moved gingerly in behind the wheelers to make the correction as he said, "Naw, it warn't drinkin'. It was just plain gaddamned carelessness, pure and simple. When I get back I'm goin' to come down over that damned corralyard boss like a swarm of bees."

The big, burly driver finished, then stepped back to yank

at his gauntlets and wag his head. Frank was not sure swarming over the corralyard boss would be the wisest course for the whip, but he said nothing and turned back to climb inside.

When the whip was on his high seat, he leaned down and said, "You all right in there? Them freight crates ain't shifted around to crowd you, have they?"

"Fine," Frank called back.

The driver eased his horses up into their collars; he was an experienced whip. There was no sudden jolt as the coach moved out. Frank raised his feet to the opposite seat, composed himself to doze, and made a little crooked grin. If the driver did not return to Guadalupe for a week, he probably would be over his indignation and would merely complain to Sam Smith about some yardman's carelessness.

Remembering the small packet tied with scarlet yarn, Frank dug it out, opened it, and had to hold his palm close to the near-side window where a cold, grayish blue tint was beginning to brighten the new day.

It was a small, golden locket, clearly of great age. It was shaped like a heart, and when he finally located the tiny clasp and opened it, there was a beautiful little painting of Antonia Medina inside.

He leaned close, gazed at the likeness for a long time, then closed the locket slowly and reached under his jacket to place the locket in a shirt pocket.

He leaned back, let go a long sigh, closed his eyes, and with his head against the back of the seat, thought of her beauty, her gentle thoughtfulness, and the fact that she had a mind of her own.

Someday, he mused to himself, he would return, and when he did, maybe they could take a long stroll up toward the old Mission on a full-moon night.

Someday—maybe next autumn. But not until he felt certain the Durans would no longer be down there. And not until he had settled the score with his uncle—Frank had recovered his money, but there remained the killing of his mother and the burning of their house.

He put a hand inside his coat against the pocket containing the little golden locket and smiled to himself again, but this time it was a different kind of smile. His uncle would have killers looking for him. They were down around Guadalupe and as Jorge Medina had said, they would also make their way up to where the burned house was. Where they would *not* be was southwesterly, down along the border where his uncle had his ranch, his business headquarters, and his big yard full of wagons, packers, warehouses, and hired hands.

The driver was cursing again, more fiercely this time. The horses were slackening off; the coach rocked and pitched a little because the roadbed was washboardy. Then it halted again. This time Frank did not alight until after the whip was on the ground, his back to Frank as he was pulling off his gauntlets and looking darkly at the fifth wheel and the part of it where the tongue was connected.

Frank walked up, leaned to follow the whip's line of sight, and could see nothing wrong, so he straightened back up and turned.

The whip was no longer blackly scowling. He was carefully folding his elegant smoke-tanned stagecoach driver's gauntlets under the shellbelt, which showed where he had opened his coat its full length.

He did not look up when Frank said, "What is it this time?"

The reply came from a heavy thicket that lined the west side of the roadbed. "This time it's you," the voice said. "Don't face around. Just unbutton your coat an' drop your gun. Mister, we're not goin' to stand out here forever. We been here long enough as it is. *Open the coat and shuck the gun!*"

Frank did not move—he scarcely even breathed until the coach driver finished folding his gloves and raised his head. "You'd better do like he says, mister. If you take a wild hair, you're not goin' to be around to see the sunrise."

Frank looked at the driver, let go a rough breath, and began unbuttoning his coat under the driver's watchful stare. "Now the weapon," the driver said, showing strong teeth worn even all along the front. "Just with the fingers, mister. That's it. Now then, hold it out at arm's length an' drop it."

CHAPTER 8

A Blood-red Dawn

THEY emerged from the underbrush at the west side of the road in cold gray dawnlight. Frank recognized the Duran brothers. Ash was in the lead, followed by Al, Pete, and a man he did not know.

Ash smiled flintily from a distance of about ten feet. He was easily six feet tall, had gray at the temples, tan-tawny, brown eyes, as did his brothers, and stood with hands hooked in his shellbelt regarding Frank Tennant in silence.

The driver looked at the wiry, dark man, who was the last one to emerge from the underbrush. "Villalobos, what you doin' out here?"

Ash finally left off staring at Frank to face the whip as he spoke. "He's earnin' his money just like you're doin'. Al, give the driver his fifty dollars." Al Duran was the youngest of the brothers. He looked to be in his late twenties or perhaps early thirties. As he counted out fifty dollars in greenbacks and handed them to the driver, Villalobos stepped closer and squinted. He was beside Ash Duran when he spoke. "It's him—I think it's him."

The oldest Duran turned his head. "You *think*?"

"It was dark. I told you that. An' I only saw him when he left the patio with old Medina. I tried to sneak closer but brushed an old headstone, which made a noise. I thought they'd hear me. I crouched down. I'm pretty sure it's him."

Ash Duran turned away as the stagecoach driver avoided Frank's eyes and climbed up the side of his coach. Al Duran yanked open the door, found the saddlebags, flung them to the ground, and slammed the door. He signaled with a raised hand, and the driver whistled up his horses.

Ash was gazing at Frank again when he said, "I *know* it's him, Villalobos."

The thin Mexican straightened back with an expression of relief. "Well then," he said, "I will go back. Chief, there is the matter of my fee."

Ash dug in a pocket, handed over some folded greenbacks, and as the Mexican was turning, said, "One other thing, Villalobos. You remember?"

"Yes. I go home to bed, and tomorrow I tell the marshal that I looked everywhere and there is no gringo in Mex town."

Pete Duran spoke to his brother. "You think you can trust him? The marshal couldn't."

Ash stood gazing dispassionately at Villalobos. The Mexican was sweating in the cold dawn. He forced a wide death's-head smile and said, "By the Holy Cross, you can trust me, Chief."

Ash jerked his head, Cruz Villalobos went hurriedly in the direction of the underbrush where the horses were tied, and as the youngest Duran handed Ash Frank's saddlebags, they could hear distinctly Villalobos riding like the wind in the direction of Guadalupe.

Visibility was steadily improving, but full daylight would not arrive for another hour or so. Frank studied the faces of the Durans. He had seen them before but never this close and never in a situation where he had spoken to any of them.

He watched Ash rummage through his saddlebags, bring forth ribbon-wrapped packets of money, and examine each packet carefully before replacing it. Finally, Ash took the heavy gold crucifix from the bottom of a saddlebag. Ash eyed it, dangled it from his hand as he raised his face and said, "It ain't all here but there's not much missing. What'd you do with it, Tennant?" Ash grinned. "I know. You paid some Mex for keepin' you safe until you could ride again. Well, I think he's better off than you are. Some time back I sent a note to your uncle that we were on your trail. You want to see the note he sent back? He said to burn your bare feet over a mesquite fire, then shoot you after you told us where his money was. We won't need no mesquite fire." Ash slung the saddlebags over a shoulder.

He swung the massive old, heavy crucifix so fast and unexpectedly that Frank had no opportunity to even turn aside. The cross hit him across the bridge of the nose and on the right cheek. Pain exploded inside his head. He raised both hands where the blood was gushing.

The Duran brothers laughed.

The noise of a light wagon coming from the north galvanized the three brothers. Two of them grabbed Tennant by the arms and followed Ash off the road into the thicket. They did not stop until they were about a hundred yards from the road. Ash and Pete went to stand with their horses to prevent noise while Al Duran pushed Frank to the ground and cocked his six-gun within inches of Frank's temple. "Not a sound," he warned.

It required a quarter of an hour for the wagon to come up and pass southward. Pete spoke softly to Ash. "Rancher." Ash nodded. When the noise was growing faint, he stepped over to where Al was holstering his weapon and knelt in front of Tennant. He leaned to drape the crucifix around Frank's neck, then leaned back smiling coldly. "Your nose don't look very good."

Frank fished for his bandanna to dab the blood. The pain was fierce. His eyes were watering profusely. He could feel the swelling. Ash's features were becoming indistinct, as if Frank was looking at him through a fish bowl.

Pete said, "Get it over with."

Ash ignored that. "Empty your pockets," he ordered Tennant.

Frank obeyed, all but his shirt pockets. Al leaned with a curse and tore the cloth to empty them. He looked at the heart-shaped locket, pried it open, squinted at the likeness of Antonia Medina, and pursed his lips in a raucous whistle. His brother Pete walked up to look also. He grinned broadly.

Only Ash remained disinterested as he pawed through the other things. "You gave us a lot of misery," he told Frank while considering Tennant's personal effects. "We been run off by cowmen, gone thirsty a couple of times, been sleepin' with sand fleas, and all the time you been livin' good in Mex town. That little runt who came out here with us knew who you were stayin' with. He also knew the whip on your coach. He took Al to meet him. Al offered him fifty dollars to stop here." Ash rocked back on his heels and raised his face. Clearly, he was enjoying himself. "It'll work out real nice. If anyone asks the whip about you when he gets back down to Guadalupe, all he's got to say is that he dropped you off up at Pinole and ain't seen you since."

Ash stood up. Al handed him the gold locket. Ash held it to the light, snapped it closed, and pocketed it. "With a nurse that pretty, a man wouldn't be in a big hurry to get well, would he? Is she the daughter of that Mex who looked after you—George Medina?"

Frank eased the big bandanna away from his face, not to reply but to see if his nose was still bleeding. It was, but not as profusely as it had been. He used one hand to shove the crucifix inside his shirt, still without looking up or speaking.

Ash snarled. "Take off your jacket and shirt."

He did not move fast enough, so Al yanked his clothes off. When Frank was naked from the waist up, the three Durans leaned to stare. As they examined his scars, Pete said incredulously, "Never thought we'd hit him that hard. How in hell did he manage to stay atop his horse shot up like that?"

Al's comment was more to the point. "How the hell did he manage to *live*?"

Ash was studying the horizon and the sky; nothing moved for as far as a man could see. There were no clouds, no wind. It was going to be a hot day. "Get him up to his feet. One of us got to ride double."

Pete turned with a bleak stare. "Do it right here, then we can get the hell out of this country."

Ash scowled. "In three days, there'll be buzzards. In five days, someone'll come to see what they're eatin'. We're goin' to take him where there's a deep arroyo—one hell of a long way from anywhere—and pile rocks on his carcass. We don't want him found."

Pete was not mollified. "What's the sense of goin' to all that work?"

Ash turned, his scowl darker. "Use your head—the marshal down there knows we're lookin' for him. If someone finds his body, that damned lawman's goin' to look for us. It don't take a lot of sense to figure it out if he's dead and we're no longer around lookin' for him—considerin' we was huntin' him high and low. Now quit your damned arguing and cinch up the horses—you can carry him behind your saddle. I want to get away from this road."

While they got the horses ready Ash began rolling a smoke. After lighting up he dug out the little gold locket, opened it, and gazed at the painting for a long time before gently closing it and putting it back into his pocket.

The pain in Frank's face had turned into a throbbing headache. His blood-stained shirt was beginning to dry stiff. As he got up into a crouch before standing erect, a little vagrant groundswell breeze rattled southward through the thicket. It provided him temporary relief from the pain as he breathed deeply through his mouth, but the breeze left as suddenly as it had arrived.

"That was a stupid thing you did," Ash said dispassionately to Frank, while considering the badly swollen nose with its purplish coloring. "You knew damned well your uncle'd never sit still until he got his money back."

"Wasn't his money," Frank mumbled.

Ash ignored that. "You worked for him. You knew as well as anyone else that he'd send someone to find you."

Frank peered from swollen eyes. "Were you up north with him?"

"You mean at your home place?"

"Yes."

"No. Us three was down in Mexico settling up with a *pronunciado* who thought he could raise an army and start a war against the Mex government. He had half his army when we caught him ridin' out with a Mex girl. We riddled him. Naw, your uncle took some of the regular hands with him when he went up there." Ash paused as one of his brothers said they were ready to ride, then he smiled at Frank again. "That darn Mex general did the same thing—he paid your uncle for three Gatling guns and two wagonloads of rifles. Then the fool sent out some of his soldiers to ambush the fellers returning with the money to your uncle. Killed 'em all and took back the money. You know, Tennant, fellers like you an' the general don't live an' learn, you just live. And since you don't learn, you don't live long."

Pete called sharply, "Someone's coming. From the south this time. Listen."

Ash straightened up and remained motionless. "Riders," he said aloud. "Keep the horses quiet. Tennant, you make a sound and I'll bust your skull like a melon."

It seemed to be a fairly large party of riders, perhaps as many as six or eight of them. Frank hoped very hard it would be someone who ran cattle in the vicinity, but even if they turned off the road westerly—unless they penetrated the underbrush, which no horseman ever did without a very good reason—they would go past as the wagon had done earlier.

But they did not turn off. They were talking about something that was very amusing to them. They laughed and hooted and made jokes while their horses plodded past the place where the stage had stopped. Evidently none of them looked down and noticed there were boot tracks in the dust.

They were still calling loudly back and forth and laughing as they rode past and kept on riding.

Ash relaxed, his hawkish, weather-bronzed features showing impatience. He gestured for Frank to go over where Pete was already mounting, then went after his own horse.

The sun was up, finally, the morning was cool and fragrant and glass clear for miles. Pete extended a grudging arm, jerked Frank up behind the saddle, removed his six-gun from its hip holster, shoved it down the front of his britches, and reined out in the wake of his two brothers who were picking their way toward the roadbed.

Ash halted briefly to look both ways, then led off across the road riding eastward.

Al, who had picked up Tennant's weapon after the stagecoach had departed, was holding the gun by the barrel as he slouched along. A couple of miles out he hauled back and hurled the weapon in a high, far arc. It landed at the base of a thick, squatty mesquite bush.

Pete unslung his canteen and drank deeply. After Pete finished, Frank asked for a drink. Pete grunted and said, "You ain't thirsty. Wait until late afternoon, then you'll be thirsty."

The morning was still cool, but in a few hours the full force of a desert sun would be burning down on them.

Ash was chewing on jerky, as he turned to consider his prisoner. "He don't look real good, Pete. Don't let him fall off."

Pete grudgingly reconsidered and passed the canteen back. Frank drank and handed the canteen back to him. Pete said, "I want that gold thing around your neck. If you give it to me now I won't have to yank it off'n your carcass later."

Frank's nose throbbed. It was terribly swollen and discolored, but the pain was much less than it had been and his headache also had lessened. He said, "I guess you'll have to get it later."

Pete shrugged. "Suit yourself. What in hell did you figure to do with all that money you stole?"

"It was mine to begin with. I wasn't goin' to do anything with it. Not for a while anyway. I had somethin' more important to do first."

"Yeah? Get a thousand miles away? He'd have found you no matter where you went."

"He wouldn't have to find me. I'd find him."

Frank felt Pete straighten in the saddle. "Find him? You mean your uncle?"

"Yeah. My uncle."

"Why?"

"Because when he stole that money he also killed my mother and burned our house down with her inside it. Can you think of any better reason?"

Pete rode a long distance in silence, then he turned his head sideways as he said, "Now I'm beginnin' to understand somethin'. He offered each of us one thousand dollars in gold double eagles to make damned sure you was dead after we caught you."

Frank was holding the cloth to his forehead when he spoke again. "An' I'll give you *three* thousand to keep on ridin' when I slip off this horse to the ground."

Pete's retort was curt. "You slip off this horse and you'll get yourself shot to pieces, then we'll drag you by the heels until Ash figures where to hide the body. Go ahead—slip off."

Frank lowered the bandanna, ignored his riding companion, and gingerly explored the bridge of his nose to determine whether or not it was broken.

CHAPTER 9

An Accident

WHERE they finally halted, with the sun high and heat haze obscuring distances, there were several spindly paloverdes growing within spitting distance of a veinlike, thin erosion gully. A horse could have jumped it; it was not very wide but it was at least eight feet deep. There were boulders down there, which had been tumbled a considerable distance. When the flash flood made that arroyo, it must have been a real gully washer. There were other such narrow, deep ditches nearby, but the one Ash stopped near had those paloverdes where horses could be tied. The other gulches lacked this convenience.

It was hot. Not unbearably so, but hot enough for the Durans to drink from their canteens as they tied up. Heat drove desert residents to cover whether they had two legs, four legs, or no legs at all.

Frank Tennant's pain was down to a dull ache. His face was badly and lopsidedly discolored. When he accepted the canteen from Pete he soaked the bandanna and after drinking raised the cloth to his upper face, where most of the soreness was, and felt instantly relieved by water made cooler by the evaporation process. He was gently massaging his eyes when Al Duran let out a squawk and jumped sideways, then fell.

Frank lowered the bandanna. Al was making whimpering sounds and pulling desperately at his left boot. When it came off he flung it aside. Both his brothers were watching in bafflement until Frank pointed at the nearby snake. "He must have been staying cool at the base of that paloverde."

It was a short, thick rattlesnake.

Ash and Pete jumped farther from the reptile, which was

69

coiled and ready to strike again. His tail was slightly raised and furiously quivering, but there were no rattles on it.

Al yelled to his brothers. Ash went over to examine the pair of small punctures and fish for his clasp knife while Pete slowly drew and aimed his six-gun. When he fired, the snake came up off the ground like a steel spring, its body blown into skin-held fragments. The snake still writhed when it came down.

Frank watched Pete stalk the dying reptile. Pete certainly knew the rattlesnake was either dying or dead when he leaned to blow the snake's head off. His second shot blew dirt, pebbles, and dust in all directions as the snake's head disintegrated.

Pete straightened up, reloaded, holstered his weapon, and finally turned. By then Ash had made two cuts on Al's lower leg where there were two punctures. One gash was directly through both fang marks. The other gash was between them.

Al was dripping sweat, his face was ashen beneath its tan, his gaze was fixed unblinkingly on the blood coming from the knife cuts. He seemed hypnotized.

Ash was kneading flesh and squeezing it toward the gashes. If venom was pushed out, no one knew it because of the blood. When Pete spoke in his detached, gruff tone the other Durans ignored him. He said, "That's the second one I seen without no tail." Being ignored by Al and Ash, he turned toward Frank Tennant. "You ever see one like that before?"

Frank hadn't and wagged his head as he watched Ash work. "No. But he was sure trying to rattle."

Pete grunted, tipped back his hat, and leaned to watch the oldest Duran, who had taken time out to twist his bandanna just below the knees of his brother as he said, "Pete, do what I was doing. Keep the blood running. Work his skin and muscles. Damn it, get down and do it!"

Pete knelt and went to work.

Frank went after a canteen, returned, and leaned to trickle water so drying blood would not cake and obscure the holes.

Time passed with no one being aware of it. Ash went to his saddlebags and returned with a pony of brandy. As he raised it for Al to drink, Pete leaned back, watched, and said, "You told me we was out of likker, Ash."

The oldest brother did not take his eyes off the youngest Duran as he replied. "It's a damned good thing I lied to you, isn't it?" He pulled the bottle back, stoppered it, and shoved it into a hip pocket with Pete watching every movement. Ash reddened. "I said keep squeezin' the flesh!"

Pete returned to his work and did not say another word until Ash eased his younger brother to the ground, rocked back and lifted a red, sweaty face to look around. "He needs shade. The damned heat'll bring on a fever."

Pete spoke sullenly without looking up from his kneading. "There ain't any. Look around. You see any shade in this godforsaken country?"

Ash eyed Pete briefly before raising his eyes to Frank Tennant. "Go pull brush until you got enough to make a ramada while Pete an' I carry him over under that paloverde tree." As Frank straightened up to turn in the direction of the nearest stand of thornpin, Ash gave him a warning. "If you try to run for it, there's no water within fifty miles an' we'll track you down before you get half that far."

Frank gazed at the older man, turned, and walked away. Both the Durans watched him briefly before lifting Al, who was beginning to look as red as a lobster and had sweat running from every pore. Even his britches were showing sweat, and his shirt was plastered to him.

Frank pulled brush. What he could not work free of the ground he left, in favor of parched old, gray dead limbs. He hauled underbrush until Ash and Pete had created an Indian shelter, using most of it overhead, pushing it among the paloverde limbs until practically no sunlight came through. Then they drank, put the canteens aside, and listened to the uneven breathing of their younger brother. When Frank dropped the last armload of faggots, Ash jerked his head for Frank to get in out of the sunlight.

As Frank resoaked the bandanna, Pete snarled, "You think them canteens is bottomless!"

Frank ignored him and leaned to squeeze the cloth so that water trickled over the fiery red and sweat-greasy face of the younger Duran. He did that three times, then gently swabbed Duran's face.

Pete was cross-legged, looking at the ground when a cooling little groundswell breeze came. His face came up. He said, "Ash, now what do we do?"

The older man held his arms out like a bird for the little breeze to reach as much of his body as it would. He did not reply until the breeze was departing and he lowered his arms. "We wait. What else can we do? Look at him. We can't move him until he quits bein' out of his head."

Pete, having expected no different answer, picked up a twig and gouged at the dirt with it. "That's goin' to be awhile. Those canteens ain't goin' to stay full forever, an' we only got enough grub in the saddlebags to last us maybe two days."

Ash dumped his hat aside and ran bent fingers through sweat-plastered hair, which was shot through with silver. "You know the answer as well as I do, Pete."

His brother nodded slightly and continued gouging with the twig. "How far is Guadalupe?"

"Maybe ten, twelve miles. You can make it down an' back in one day if you start before sunup in the morning."

Pete tossed the stick aside. "Me?"

Ash made a flinty smile. "Yeah. Unless you want to flip a coin."

Pete pushed sweat off his forehead with a grimy sleeve and squinted dead ahead as he said, "All right. Before dawn tomorrow." He turned to gaze at Al, and Frank who was sitting beside the injured man. "How's he look, Tennant?"

"Like someone who's been snakebit. He sucks air in fits and starts, mumbles, sometimes opens his eyes and looks like he's conscious." Frank gazed steadily at Pete. He disliked them all. They were cruel, merciless men, but Pete, in Frank's opinion, would have ridden off and left his brother. Ash, the man who had viciously struck out with the heavy old crucifix, had been very protective of his injured sibling. Perhaps it was as Frank's mother had told him: there is no such thing as a thoroughly bad individual. But when he looked at Pete Duran he concluded his mother probably had been wrong. From what he now knew of the Durans, men with very bad reputations, Ash might be able to qualify, but Frank doubted very much that Pete Duran was not completely bad.

They went out to care for their animals. What the horses needed more than shade and feed was water. They were tucked up. But there was no water for them, and if Ash had been telling the truth, there was no water closer than a long day's ride.

While they were out there, Frank eyed Al Duran's holstered Colt, held in place by a plaited tie-down thong. He looked from the shady place out yonder where Ash and Pete were dumping saddles and bridles after hobbling the animals. Both men were too far away for him to see them distinctly.

He could risk going for Al's gun but decided not to. Not now anyway. When they were closer, sitting disconsolately under the brush shelter, his chances would be much better, and of one thing he was dead certain—if he could get Al's gun in his hand, he would have to shoot fast and accurately because they would not let him survive if he did not kill them first.

He sighed, watched them walking back, gingerly felt his lopsided, badly discolored face, particularly felt his nose, which was not broken after all, and as the Durans crouched over to get into the shade, he felt for the damp bandanna to work some remaining caked blood off his face.

In a moment of silence Al suddenly said, "Ash, he'll tell

the marshal. If he would double-cross Bierk, he'll double-cross us."

His brothers twisted to stare and listen, then slowly turned forward again. "Out of his head," Ash mumbled.

Pete ignored that. "It's the truth."

Ash was not worried. "All right. Bierk'll play hell finding us out here."

That brought Pete's head up. In an indignant tone he said, "What the hell are you talkin' about? All Bierk's got to do is make up a posse, ride north where the stage stopped, pick up our tracks, and ride right up to this damned tree." When Pete paused for breath he began to scowl at his brother. "You go down there tomorrow. If Villalobos told Bierk we caught him headin' for Bierk's place and made him tell us where Tennant was and who was drivin' that coach, if any one of us shows up in Guadalupé tomorrow, that lawman's goin' to skin him alive."

Ash looked under his sleeve for a crawling dog tick, removed it, got it positioned atop one thumbnail, and ground it to death under the other thumbnail. As he was flicking the tiny body away he said, "Maybe by morning we can move Al. If he can't ride, one of us can balance him from each side."

Pete thought about that as he peered from slitted eyes out where the horses were listlessly lipping at protected grass growing in close to the base of thornpin bushes. "If this hadn't happened, we'd have been to water by now. Look at them horses—by noon tomorrow they'll be stumbling. By evening we'll be leadin' 'em."

Ash's temper flared. "All right. What d'you want to do?"

Pete made a slashing rearward gesture with one thick arm. "Shoot Tennant, dump him down into that gully, get astride, and try to make it southeast to water before we're afoot."

Ash looked coldly at his brother and said, "Why in hell couldn't that snake have bit you? Pete, I could kill Tennant like you said without even lookin' back. But we're not goin' to leave Al."

Frank saw the look on Ash Duran's face. He had not looked that coldly savage, even when he'd struck Frank with the crucifix. Frank breathed shallowly, awaiting Pete's reply, but there was none.

As Ash's wrath dwindled, he eventually said, "All right, I'll go to Guadalupe. You and Tennant stay with the kid. Head for that spring we found last month. When I can I'll head over there from Guadalupe. And Pete, you'll need Tennant to help hold Al on his horse."

Al opened his eyes and struggled to sit up. Frank swung quickly to brace him, then eased him gently back to the ground. Al was panting like a dog, so Frank trickled water into his mouth. He choked, swallowed, then stiffened to push upright again. Frank put one hand on his chest. Al's eyes bulged; he was looking toward the brassy sky with an unfocusing stare.

The spasm only lasted a moment or two. Afterward Al turned limp again with sweat running like water. Frank got his head slightly raised and trickled more liquid from the canteen. Al drank, then fainted.

Pete frowned at Frank. "You ever see anyone rattlesnake-bit before?"

"Cattle and horses. A dog once, but never a man. But like everyone else, I've been listenin' to stories about rattlesnake bites since I was a kid."

Pete squared around, not interested in what Frank had heard. He had heard the same stories. So had Ash. So had just about everyone else who lived in rattlesnake country. The commonly accepted antidote was whiskey. They had none. There were a few swallows left in Ash's pony of brandy, but since Ash made no move toward his saddlebags, Frank had to guess that Ash would use the brandy only if his brother seemed to need it worse than he seemed to need it right now.

The sun moved, something none of them cared about

until it got so low in the west that its slanting rays came into their shaded place from the side, below the shielding faggots.

Pete rummaged in the saddlebags for something to eat. Ash made him divide the jerky, sardines, and horsesweat-tasting tortillas wrapped around frijoles. Not a word was said as they chewed. The only thing that did not require a lot of masticating was the sardines. Few rangemen liked them, but there were two reasons why they carried them: the tins were flat so they fit well in saddlebags, and the oil kept thirst from bothering a man all night if he ate them for supper, and for most of the day otherwise.

When they finished, Ash wordlessly piled what remained of their food on the ground. By Frank's estimate there was enough for two more meals. Ash looked at his brother. "Divvy it," he said.

Pete nodded without meeting Ash's gaze.

"If Al comes around, you'n Tennant get some of that fish oil down him. Maybe it'll work like medicine."

Al Duran was red-faced, soaked with sweat, and unconscious. The leg that had been slashed in an attempt to get the poison out was swollen and purple mottled.

Ash stood a long moment gazing downward, then turned away to rummage in his saddlebag for the depleted pony of brandy, which he took back and handed to Frank. "If you figure he needs it, pour some down him," he said, and walked over to his seated brother. They eyed each other.

After a moment Ash said, "I know what you're thinkin'."

Pete's reply was short. "What about it?"

Ash said, "Don't shoot him if there's a chance the two of you can hold Al in the saddle as far as the spring."

A short while later when desert dusk had turned to near-darkness in a matter of minutes, Ash lugged his outfit toward the hobbled animals.

He had been gone for about half an hour when foraging coyotes sounded, sometimes yapping on the run, sometimes sitting back to howl. They had probably picked up the scent of blood and food.

CHAPTER 10

Nightrider's Moon

THERE was a slow-rising moon, three-quarters full and capable of bringing the landscape to a pewterlike brightness.

Pete had a plug, which he gnawed on then shoved back into a shirt pocket. He faced Frank as he tongued the cud into his cheek. The coyotes went on, their night-long hunt continuing.

Frank's injuries no longer hurt unless he touched them, but he was tired to the bone, no longer able to support the fear that had been with him all day, so he gazed back at Pete Duran wearily and resignedly. Pete was, if not the worst of the Durans, then at least the most callous. He jutted his jaw in the direction of his brother and said, "He's not goin' to make it."

Frank looked down briefly at the grease-shiny face. "He might. I've heard that about as many folks survive as die from rattler venom."

Pete spat, ranged a long look at his brother, spat again, and twisted to reach for a canteen. While he was facing away, Frank darted furtive fingers to yank loose the tie-down holding Al Duran's gun in its holster.

Faced forward, Pete tipped the canteen to drink and watched Frank with one eye until he lowered the canteen. Then he capped it and tossed it aside. "You think Ash'll make it down there and get away with some food?"

Frank, who had listened to Duran swallowing water and had afterward watched the man toss the canteen aside, knew better than to say he was thirsty. "He's got a good chance if he gets down there in the dark."

Pete changed the subject. "How much did you pay that Mexican to hide you?"

"Nothing."

"You damned liar."

"Count the money."

Pete turned aside, got heavily to his feet, and walked over where their riding gear was jumbled together. Frank Tennant watched Pete while reaching slowly for the younger brother's weapon.

Pete suddenly jumped, waved his arms, and swore loudly. "It's gone. That son of a bitch took those saddlebags with him!"

Frank drew his hand back slowly. Pete was too agitated to notice; the moonlight wasn't strong enough under the brush shelter for him to see what Frank had been doing. "Did you see him take them saddlebags, Tennant?"

"No. Are you sure?"

Pete turned to kick viciously among the saddles, blankets, and bridles. "Look," he snarled. "You see them? They're gone. They was here when we dumped the outfits. They sure as hell never walked away." Pete swung to glare southward in the direction his brother had taken.

Frank started to reach for the holstered Colt again.

Pete let go with a string of curses, turned back, and stamped over to the shelter. His face was twisted and almost black, but when he spoke his voice was quiet. "You know why he did that? Damn his soul to hell! He did it because he figured as soon as he was out of hearin' I'd shoot you, toss you down into that arroyo, saddle up, an' leave Al to make it or die on his own."

Frank did not move or make a sound, but he thought Pete was probably right. If he was, then Ash Duran knew his brother inside and out. Frank had not had time to think about it but now that he did, he believed Ash had probably saved Al's life and Frank's by taking the saddlebags.

Pete leaned down and thrust out his right hand. "Give me that bottle."

Frank saw his chance, but hung fire. If he succeeded it would be almighty close. A better chance might arrive later. His delay rekindled Pete Duran's fury. He snarled a curse and balled the outstretched hand. Frank saw him draw it back and rocked sideways. Pete missed. He was not really balanced for what he had attempted, so he got his feet into a better position and with teeth bared let out a snarl and launched himself at Tennant.

This time there was no way to escape. Frank was sitting on the ground. Al Duran was behind him lying out his full length. In the half second Frank had to react, he did so without thinking. He rocked forward as though to arise but there was no time, nor was that his intention. He would have one chance and not another one. His body dropped on one side as his right arm came up. He was concentrating with everything he had on Pete's face when he fired his right fist, twisting his upper body in behind the blow.

The sound was like a falling horse, muted but with noticeable reverberations. Pete Duran's entire body was knocked sideways. He stumbled over his unconscious brother and was desperately trying to break his fall when Frank unwound up off the ground, bringing Al's six-gun with him.

Pete rolled sideways; there was blood on his lower face. The blow would have staggered a horse and flattened most men. Duran's movements were instinctive but sluggish. His savage look was gone, his eyes were popped wide open, he did not appear to realize his mouth had been smashed by that blow. He had his gun butt gripped in one hand when Frank cocked the weapon he was aiming and said, "Leave the gun be. Take your hand away from it."

Possibly Pete was dazed, just as possibly he did not hear the order. He got the six-gun clear of leather as Frank stepped over Al, aimed a kick at the rising gun, missed it, but caught Pete's elbow with enough force to half fling Duran sideways. The gun rose from his hand, sailed beyond the shelter, and fell to the ground.

Frank knelt to push Al's cocked Colt against Pete's neck. "That's enough."

Pete rolled to hold his injured elbow with his free hand, and rocked back and forth. He was not facing Frank and made no attempt to. The pain was bad enough to make him groan behind clenched teeth.

Frank stood up, eased the hammer down, let the gun hang at his side as he watched. Behind them Al made a gutteral cough, reached out with both hands to gouge at the hardpan earth with bent fingers. This only lasted a few moments, then the youngest Duran turned loose all over.

After Pete sat up—shirt torn, hat gone, dirt on his face, still rocking as he clutched his injured elbow—Frank said, "Get over on your belly, face down."

He stared without moving or making a sound. Frank raised the gun slowly and repeated: "Face down!"

Pete still rocked and held his arm. "You son of a bitch," he said hoarsely, and lowered his face to look left and right for his gun.

Frank leaned, and without great force, struck the injured man over the head with his gun barrel. Pete crumpled so that Frank had to toe him over, face down in the dirt, before yanking Pete's belt loose to lash his ankles, then pull both arms in back and tie them using two bandannas, one his own, the other one Pete's. He arose after rolling Pete face up.

Al Duran's breathing was bubbly and irregular.

Frank shoved the gun into his empty holster, stepped over for one of the canteens, knelt to raise Al and pour water down him. A little went down, the rest filled Al's mouth until it trickled out both sides. Frank worked the gullet to make Al swallow. Nothing happened.

He put the canteen aside, eased Al down, and leaned over him. The youngest Duran was dead.

The night was silent. The remaining two tucked-up saddle

animals were dozing, indistinct but recognizable dark shapes out a short distance.

Frank tilted a canteen, drank his fill, and hefted the canteen to estimate how much water remained in it. Then he stepped back over to Pete, hoisted him, ignored the trickle of blood coming through his hair down his forehead. After Frank got him positioned against one leg, he held the canteen above him. He did not use much water.

Pete sputtered, turned his head away, and strained against his bindings.

Frank stoppered the canteen, put it aside, and said, "Can you hear me?"

The answer was part groan. "My arm's broke. Untie it. It hurts like hell."

Frank dragged Pete close to the trunk of a paloverde tree and propped him there. He did not untie the injured arm. "Listen to me," he said. "Your brother is dead. You hear me?"

Pete turned his head slowly to gaze at the inert, flattening shape of his younger brother, then turned back to face Tennant. His mouth was no longer bleeding, but it was badly enough swollen to make it a little difficult to understand what he said when he spoke. "Untie my goddamn arm, Tennant."

"I said your brother is dead."

"I heard you. Untie my goddamn arm."

Frank squatted facing his prisoner.

Pete's face did not look any better than Frank's face. They eyed one another in the pleasant desert night. Frank was still tense, but the man he had beaten seemed bothered only by his arm. His breathing was normal again, his eyes focused, there was caked blood on his swollen mouth, but Frank had to be impressed with the man's inherent toughness.

Pete suddenly said, "Listen. You know what my brother's goin' to do? He's not goin' to Guadalupe. Not with thirty thousand dollars on the saddle with him. He's runnin' off. Far away. To some place where he's never been before."

Frank remained silent. He did not entirely doubt Pete, but he had been impressed all afternoon and into the night with Ash's genuine concern for his younger brother. Perhaps if Ash knew his little brother was dead, he would do exactly as Pete had just said, but he didn't know that.

Of one thing Frank had been certain: Ash Duran's concern was genuine. Frank wagged his head and arose, looking out where the dozing horses were. "I don't think so, Pete. I think he'll head for that spring. You just sit comfortable while I bring in the horses and rig them out."

Pete's features puckered. "We're goin' to Guadalupe?"

"No. We're goin' to that spring. You're goin' to guide us there."

As Frank scooped up a couple of ropes and strode in the direction of the horses, Pete Duran watched him with a puzzled expression. About the time Frank had the horses and was leading them back, Pete's face cleared. "The money," he muttered to himself. "He's goin' to lay an ambush for Ash an' get the money back."

Frank's strength had been recovering since they had eaten. But it was still all he could manage to get the flopping, inert body of Al Duran across a saddle and lash it there. Pete yelled at him. "Are you crazy? We may need that horse. Fifty miles is a hell of a distance on rode-down and tucked-up animals. Leave Al here. It's not goin' to make a damned bit of difference to him."

Frank continued to work with the animals as though he had not heard a word. But when he finished and started over to hoist Pete to his feet, he said, "Did you three grow up together?"

Pete stifled an outcry as he was roughly yanked up to his feet. "That arm's killin' me, Tennant. Untie it. What can I do with a busted arm an' no weapons?"

"Did the three of you grow up together?"

"Yeah. In a mud town over along the New Mexico-Texas border."

Frank gave him a slight shove in the direction of the horses. "I got another question for you, Pete. Did you ever care about anyone in your life?"

Duran replied through clenched teeth, which made him even harder to understand. "Yeah. I care about that gun back there and every good horse I ever rode." He stopped beside his animal and dug in his heels. "I'm goin' to tell you something, Tennant. You can shoot me right here, but I'm not gettin' on that horse unless you untie my arm. You try boostin' me up there an' I'll balk like a bay steer. Go ahead an' try it."

Frank untied Duran's arms. As Pete swung them forward, he had to strangle an outcry. He gasped like someone who had just jumped into an ice-cold creek. "Jesus! The bones are grindin' against one another. You bastard—you broke it. Where is that brandy?"

Frank turned to scuff in the dust until he found the little bottle. He opened it, raised it, considered its contents, then held it out.

Pete grabbed it with his good hand and tipped his head far back. Frank yanked the bottle away and held it up again. Pete had downed half of what had been in the bottle. Frank said, "Get on your horse."

He went over to Al's animal, swung up behind the cantle, shoved the little bottle inside his shirt, and with someone's Winchester carbine in one hand, reins in the other hand, he told Pete to take the lead. He also told him there had never been a man born nor a horse foaled who could outrun a bullet, but that he was welcome to try to be the first if he felt like it.

Pete rode with his broken arm shoved inside the front of his shirt. He was clearly in bad pain. After a few miles he tried to cradle the arm in his lap, but that was not a success because the horse rocked along as he walked.

Once Pete looked back. "This pain is real bad, Tennant. Let's stop and fashion me a bandage of some kind."

Frank motioned with the saddle gun. "Keep riding and shut up."

"Well, let me have the rest of the brandy then."

"I told you to shut up. The next time I won't tell you anything. I'll bust your backbone too. Where is this spring we're heading for?"

"East a fair distance and south. We come onto it by accident. There was an old Mexican driving some goats along. We saw him from a little hill and figured he'd know where there was water. He led us straight to the spring. I'd guess it's about twenty or so miles almost due east of Guadalupe."

"What else did the old Mexican know?"

"Nothing. He looked scairt pea green when the three of us rode up to him."

"Was the other one scairt, the one that fixed things so's you could catch me on that stage?"

"Villalobos? That lawman down there had hired him to sneak around in Mex town to find you. He saw you and some old Mex walkin' back from a church. Ash, Al, and I was in town after dark for a few drinks at the saloon when we saw him sneakin' around over at the jailhouse. The light was burnin' in the office, but Marshal Bierk wasn't there. The Mex looked real upset about that. Ash had a hunch, so we went over and caught him from three sides."

"What did he tell you?"

"That he'd snuck up to the shack of that Mex who was hidin' you and heard him an' you talkin' about how you would take the first stage out of Guadalupe. My idea was to grab you right in the corralyard, but Ash had a better idea. It sure worked too, didn't it?"

Frank agreed, but not out loud.

Pete cut across his bitter thoughts. "I told Ash we should shoot Villalobos. Sure as hell no matter how much money we gave him, that kind of son of a bitch would sell out to the marshal just as soon as he got back to town. He'd collect twice, maybe get us caught by Bierk, an' everyone would be in trouble but him. Ash didn't even listen to me. I'll tell you what I think, Tennant. If Bierk don't catch Ash in Guadalupe, it'll be because he's not in town. He's back yonder somewhere tryin' to track us by moonlight."

Frank said, "I hope so. How much farther?"

Pete did not answer because he was trying to cradle his arm in some new position to lessen the pain.

CHAPTER 11

A Bad Time

BY the time there was a chill to the night, the moon had been gone a long while. Frank Tennant had to concentrate on moving things: his horse's ears, Pete Duran a few yards ahead, Duran's horse, the flopping corpse across the saddle seat directly in front.

It wasn't drowsiness—he was seeing things. Once it was a band of horsemen approaching like ghosts in the starlight. Another time it was a big dog-wolf loping along beside the horse, tongue lolling, head low.

He raised the brandy bottle. There were about two swallows left. He drank them and pitched the little bottle aside. Where it landed, starlight made a faint reflection.

Up ahead, Pete Duran rode with his head hanging forward as though he were sleeping, but he wasn't sleeping either. He was being tortured by pain arising with every step of his mount.

The horses were dragging their hind hooves, making scuff marks. They moved mechanically, putting their hooves down, raising them a few inches, then putting them down again. They, too, were on the verge of losing touch with reality. For them the hardship was worse; they were larger—there was more body area to suffer from dehydration.

Brandy was something Tennant had tasted before but had never cared for. Especially the kind that burned like fire. He did not care for it now, but it accomplished something for him whiskey probably would not have accomplished. He began to see things more clearly; the phantoms which had bothered him earlier no longer did. He felt a subtle change in the horse under him. Its head came up, little ears pointing ahead.

Duran's horse, with half the burden of Tennant's animal, reacted even more excitedly, and Duran swore at it through swollen lips. But moments later, he too raised his head.

Frank Tennant had had this experience with horses before. They smelled water. He looked around. The country looked the same—rough, with flinty poor soil, an occasional palo-verde, some catclaw cactus, here and there dusty-appearing, man-high bushes, gullies, and pale clumps of bunchgrass.

If they had reached the spring, both Ash and Pete had been wrong. There was no way he and Pete could have covered fifty miles on staggering horses in one night. Duran muttered something in a croak that Frank could not understand. He kneed his horse up beside Duran and scowled. Duran jutted his jaw like an Indian. "Yonder. Can you make out them big green bushes?"

Tennant made them out. "Yeah. That's the spring?"

"Yes."

Duran turned a stubbly face with sunken, venomous eyes. Because starlight made dark places beneath his cheekbones and around his slit of a mouth with its swollen, scabbed-over lips, he looked like a personification of evil as he said, "That's the spring. I recognize them bushes. Let me have what's left of that brandy."

"I drank it."

Duran let go an unsteady long breath. "My arm's swole as big as a flour sack."

The horses were lifting their feet now because the ground over which they were walking was spongy. There was grass, cropped short but, nevertheless, grass. And there were dense and flourishing stands of underbrush that had to be plowed through before they reached the soggy place with running water in the middle of it.

Duran got down and dropped to the ground, leaving Frank to fight the thirst-crazed animals. He let each one have five big swallows, then yanked them back. When they resisted, he gave each animal a kick.

He ignored Pete Duran, who was rocking again, cradling his swollen and discolored arm. It required almost an entire hour of letting the horses have a few swallows at a time before he could get them away to be tied. If they'd tanked up all at one time, they'd have been foundered.

Getting Al to the ground was easier than loading him. He slid down Tennant like a snake and lay unnaturally crumpled at his feet. As Frank was bending over to straighten Al out with both arms across his stomach, Pete croaked for a canteen. Frank emptied one of stale water, refilled it at the spring, and took it over to the injured man. Duran drank deeply but could not stopper the canteen, so he handed it to Frank, who stoppered it and left Pete to go stand where he could distantly make out the horizon. There was no sign of dawn over there, but it had to be appearing soon.

Frank went to the spring, removed his shirt, and washed, holding cupped handfuls of cold water to his lacerated and feverish face. He continued to do this until Pete called to him. "Hey. You know anythin' about settin' bones?"

Frank flung his soaked hair back, dumped the old hat back into place, picked up his shirt, and walked back. He knew something about setting bones—as much as any rangeman would know—but that knowledge did not include anything but clean breaks in mid-length, like an arm or a leg. Not an elbow.

He squatted, took Duran's arm, and started to gently straighten it. Pete almost came up off the ground with a howl and used his good hand to shove Tennant's hand off. "What're you tryin' to do?" he stormed through torn lips. "I told you—it's broke right where you kicked me."

Frank settled back on his heels. "Nothing I can do," he stated.

Pete balefully regarded Tennant, then felt his face with his good hand and unexpectedly grinned. This tore loose some of the scabs, and his split lips bled a little. "You know what you look like, Tennant? Your face's lopsided. Your nose is thicker through the middle than my wrist. You're the ugliest lookin' man I ever seen."

Frank faintly grinned back. "You're a mess, Duran. And your mouth is beginnin' to bleed again."

Pete eyed the six-gun in Tennant's holster. "That thing's got a filed spring. Al dang near shot his foot off one time with it. That's what scairt the whey out of me last night when you aimed it at me." He looked over where his brother was and gently wagged his head. "Al never used his head in his damned life. He'd hear about somethin' like havin' his gun fixed to fire at the brush of a finger over the trigger, an' right away he had to have his gun fixed that way." Pete continued to gaze at the dead man. "He was the youngest y'know. When our maw and paw upped and died, Ash was full grown, I was mostly grown, but Al . . ." Duran's sunken eyes came back to Frank's face. "You ever know a grown man who still thought and acted like a little kid? That was Al. Ash mothered him like an old settin' hen. I told him one time he'd ought to get himself a woman and raise a batch of youngsters of his own to fret over." Pete raised his good hand to the left side of his face. "He hit me so hard I thought he'd busted my jaw." Duran lowered the hand slowly, shifted his fierce eyes slightly to the right of Tennant's head, and said, "Listen."

Frank heard nothing but the occasional whiplike sound as one of the limbs of the underbrush snapped back after one of the horses had stripped it of leaves.

"You hear it?" Duran said. He had his knees pulled up, the injured arm positioned across them against his chest. It was the only position he had found that lessened the pain. "Tennant, you hear that?"

"No."

Pete's teeth showed in the darkness of his stubbly, haggard face. "Ash comin' back. Listen. Hey, Tennant . . ."

Frank was already standing up, looking into the chilly, southwesterly darkness. He had finally heard it—not the sound of a walking horse, but the noise it made when it blew its nose.

He rested a palm upon the jutting butt of Al Duran's weapon. Pete saw this and looked frantically in the direction of the oncoming horse, threw his head back, and bellowed.

"Ash! Tennant's got a gun!"

Frank turned but it was too late. Duran was looking up at him with another wolfish grin.

The sounds of that horse stopped completely, but the tied animals had heard it, or had smelled it—they were twisting as far as they could on their tie-shanks peering in the direction of the earlier sounds. One horse fidgeted, scuffed dirt and swung left and right before whinnying.

Frank dropped the shirt, ran for cover, got behind a wide stand of something with tiny leaves like mesquite but which smelled faintly like musk, and hunkered down, gun in hand.

He had left the Winchester he had been carrying all night over by dead Al Duran. Only for a moment did he regret this. If that was Ash out there, and they backed and filled through the underbrush looking for one another, the shooting would be at close range. Frank would not need the Winchester. In fact it would be an impediment.

Pete was yelling again, and strangely, while it was difficult to understand him in his normal tone, when he yelled the words were distinct. They also carried well in the otherwise total stillness.

"Ash! He ducked into the underbrush behind me. Across from the spring. He's got Al's gun. Look sharp. The son of a bitch busted my arm an' got Al's weapon. Be real careful."

After Pete's last echo died there was not a sound. There had been no answering yell to any of Pete's shouts. There was not one now.

Frank's naked upper body felt the predawn chill. He was only distantly conscious of this as he eased down to burrow as soundlessly as he could into the underbrush. In daylight, movement would have betrayed him. In the faintly diminishing cold darkness, quivering branches would only have been noticeable if his adversary were very close, and that was one thing Frank felt confident was not the case.

Wherever Ash Duran was, his visibility would be as limited as Frank's was. Tennant did not go hunting for Ash. He wanted Duran to come hunting him. Sooner or later, because the area of the spring was not very large—no more than about an acre and a half—if Ash felt impelled to settle with Tennant before moving closer to his surviving brother, he would have to clear Tennant out as a threat. He couldn't do this by remaining over yonder somewhere with his horse.

As far as Frank was concerned, this was going to be Ash Duran's game. Frank was not going to move. He did not have to. If Ash wanted to get to Pete and their horses, he would have to move to do it. All Frank had to do was lie like a lizard deep in the thicket with spiky limbs scratching his back, drawing blood, and wait.

Pete garrulously cried out again. "Arm's broke, I need some whiskey for the pain, and I'm starving. Al died back yonder, an' that darned idiot Tennant brought him over here with us. Hurry up and get him, Ash. I need somethin' for the pain."

Frank's rosary got caught on several wiry little limbs. After extricating it, he removed the rosary from around his neck and shoved it into a trouser pocket, then gripped the six-gun and tried to detect a sound. He had no idea from which direction he would be stalked, but he was reasonably certain Ash Duran would be unable to see him in his hiding place. At least for as long as the darkness remained.

It did not occur to him until he had been hiding like a lizard deep in the scratchy thicket for a quarter of an hour that Ash Duran might be doing the same thing—waiting for Frank to come to him.

It sure as hell had to be something like that, otherwise by

now he would have at the very least heard something. Despite the chill, Frank was sweating.

Pete had been silent for a long time. Maybe that was significant and maybe it wasn't. Curiosity made Frank twist to begin working his way toward Pete very carefully. The distance was actually no more than perhaps a hundred feet, but easing back little limbs, then slithering ahead and easing them back again was a slow, painstaking process. The alternative would be to move fast, make noise, cause the tops of the underbrush to wigwag, and probably get shot.

He was sacrificing his initiative. As long as he had been patiently motionless, Ash would eventually have had to come to him if he hoped to get his surviving brother away before daylight.

By the time he was close enough to see the tethered horses, which were close to Pete Duran, on his left, the world was beginning to softly brighten. There was also a faint fragrance of musky-smelling wildflowers. Frank was belly down, looking along the ground at Pete Duran's left side. Pete was still sitting with both knees drawn up to cradle and support his injured arm. It looked awkward and probably was, but if that was the only way for Pete to get relief from the pain, he had reason to do it.

Movement across from Pete, in front but over where weak lavender dawnlight did not penetrate well, caught and held Frank's attention. Pete was also staring fixedly in that direction.

Frank's nerves crawled. He had expected Ash to stalk him from over on the farther west side of the spring, where he had first heard the sound of Duran's arrival. Now, when a man's arm appeared using a Winchester to ease aside the thicket, Frank settled his gun hand into position, aiming directly at that thicket. The Winchester and the arm were gone. There was not a sound.

Frank glanced once at Pete. It was barely light enough now to make out the injured man's face. Pete seemed tense.

Frank's impression was that Pete had expected his brother to settle with Frank first. The hint of angry exasperation on Pete's face could just as easily have been the result of his long wait and the pain.

There was a long period of stillness. Frank flicked away two dog ticks—at least he hoped they were dog ticks, not fever ticks. A fist-sized, hairy tarantula appeared two feet ahead. It raised up on its legs, staring malevolently at Frank, who risked movement by pitching dirt and small stones. The tarantula left, heading in Pete's direction.

Frank looked around, then settled down to wait, and watched Pete. He suddenly had a disturbing thought.

Suppose Ash's plan was to simply lie there until visibility returned, then systematically ground sluice the area behind his brother where Pete had warned him Tennant had gone?

He scarcely had time to consider this when the saddle-gun barrel appeared again, lifted high to ease aside wiry limbs across from Pete, but more southward this time. Now, there was adequate light for Frank to take aim by. He caught occasional glimpses of a thick body writhing its way through the underbrush over there.

Remembering what Pete had said about the hair trigger on Al's gun, Frank moved his hand very slowly, thumb hooked over the hammer, ready to cock the thing but unwilling to do it until a second or two before he fired.

He heard Pete gasp, a sound as loud as someone pulling a horseshoe rasp over wood. That loud and as scratchy. It diverted Frank for a moment, then he swung his stare back to the man in the opposite stand of brush. The man's hat, head, shoulders, and part of his torso were visible. He had the Winchester tucked firmly into the flesh of his shoulder, aiming squarely at Pete.

Frank saw half the man's face. *It was not Ash Duran!*

CHAPTER 12

Bud Shilling's Revelation

IN this life there were three certainties: death, trouble, and when a man aimed at another man with a saddle gun from a distance of a hundred and fifty feet, then cocked his weapon, he was going to shoot.

Even as Frank eased the hammer back on Al Duran's touchy hand gun, he was thinking that something about that half-hidden gunman was vaguely familiar. Then he fired.

The carbine rose higher than the underbrush and fell back through a gout of desert dust. Frank could not believe he had missed at that distance. Later, he would assuage his shame by blaming it on the tricky light. Until he knew better.

The man who'd had dirt flung in his face was scrambling away with the haste of an injured bear, and he made almost as much noise.

Pete Duran must have forgotten about his arm because he whipped half around. He could see a man flat on the ground, but there was too much underbrush to see him very well. Pete did not have to see Frank's face; he could see part of his upper body. It was shirtless.

Pete was so stunned his mouth was sagging open.

Across the way where that man had disappeared, someone called softly. The name came into the hush following the echo of Frank's muzzleblast very clearly. "What the hell! Smith?"

There was no answer and no more noise. Pete swallowed, spat, and spoke quietly to Frank. "You missed him, for cris'sake. I could hit a toad left-handed with a rock at that distance. You know who he was?"

Frank didn't. "No."

"Sam Smith. Now you know?"

Frank stopped watching for movement and peered out at Pete. "The corralyard boss down at Guadalupe?"

"Yeah."

Frank relaxed against the gritty earth. "I thought it was Ash."

Pete faced forward watching the underbrush where the man with the Winchester had been. "He was goin' to shoot me. I hardly even know him."

Frank's thoughts were on a different topic. If someone from Guadalupe was out here, then there were probably more of them, maybe a posse. If it was the town marshal with riders, he had sure as hell done what Pete had been so upset about back where Al had died. He had tracked Duran and Tennant by moonlight.

Frank let the gun hang loose in his fist. Whatever the corralyard boss was doing out here, by himself or with a posse, he had made one thing very clear—he was not above shooting an unarmed, injured man.

He said, "Sit still and be quiet," to Pete Duran, and began squirming backward. It was difficult, there was no place to turn around, his naked back got scraped again by wiry little, thorny limbs, and he could not move as fast as he wanted to.

Whoever was over yonder across the spongy area of the spring knew Pete was not alone. Whether it was one man or ten men, they would start stalking the man who had almost hit Sam Smith.

Frank panted with his mouth wide open in order not to make noise as he breathed hard from exertion. By the time he got back where he had started from, dawn was spreading. It was still shadowy in the underbrush, but it would not stay that way long.

If the corralyard boss would shoot one man, there was a good chance that he would shoot another one. All Frank could recall about Sam Smith was that he had a hard face and piercing eyes. Possibly, as Antonia had told him during one of their discussions while he had been recovering, most of the men who lived and worked in Guadalupe had come to the South Desert from somewhere else, usually a long way off, and so it was said in Mex town, had been on their way over the line down into Mexico for reasons of personal health when they had decided to linger in Guadalupe.

If anyone could have convinced Frank Tennant of this, it would have been about fifteen minutes ago when he had watched Sam Smith deliberately aim at Pete Duran, who could not run and was not armed.

There was not a doubt in Tennant's mind that the corral-yard boss had intended to kill Duran.

Finally back where he could squirm around facing east, Frank sat up, brushed gravel and dirt off his sweaty body, ignored the little bleeding scratches, and wished he had one of the canteens.

He listened, but if they were hunting him, they had removed their spurs. It took a little time for Frank to get his breath back. He used it shucking out the load he had fired from the Duran gun and plugging in another one from his shellbelt. Then he raised the gun, turned it from side to side, and sighted down the barrel. He lowered it and raised it three times to look down the barrel. Maybe it hadn't been the tricky light that had made him miss—there was a deep score on one side of the barrel. He lowered the gun to his lap. His shot had gone to the right. A gunsmith with the proper instruments would be able to determine if the barrel had been bent. It would not take more than a fraction of misalignment for the gun to fire to the right.

Frank leathered the weapon, fished for his old bandanna, and mopped at his face with it as he speculated how the gun had got that bruise on the barrel back within a couple of inches of the cylinder. Pete had contemptuously disparaged his younger brother, and right now Frank was inclined to believe that at least Al had not taken very good care of the gun he'd had modified with a hair trigger.

A faintly abrasive sound in back, toward the grassy place around the spring but closer to the underbrush, made Frank hold his breath for a moment, then begin to twist from the waist very slowly as he reached for the Duran gun.

He could see out through the underbrush better than someone else could see in. His heart faltered. It was not a man, it was three men spread out to the left and right, with cocked Winchesters. As if that wasn't frightening enough, around in front of his hiding place someone rode up on a horse and spoke without raising his voice.

"Come out. Leave the gun behind and crawl out of there. If you don't, we're goin' to chop that brush flat down with lead, an' with you in the middle of it. You hear me?"

Frank's throat was as dry as cotton. He turned very slowly to look for the mounted man, saw the horse and its rider's legs but no more.

The same quiet voice spoke again. "You don't have the chance of a snowball in hell. You got five seconds. That's all."

There was no alternative. He had been caught like a bug in the middle of a spider web. "All right. I'm coming out."

"Leave the gun."

"All right."

He crawled to the edge of the brush, got up onto all fours, and looked up. The man on the horse was aiming a cocked six-gun. He was large without the heavy coat—with it he looked as big as a bear. He ordered Frank to stand up, then the gun in his gloved fist sagged a little as he looked at the bloody, battered, gaunt and sunken-eyed man who was standing shirtless before him. He wagged his head, eased down the hammer, leathered his Colt and called out, "All right. Come on around behind the bushes. I got him."

Someone called back in a surly voice. "What about this one? He's got a busted arm an' looks like someone hit him in the face with a fence slat."

"One of you stay with him. Rest of you come around here. Bring that old shirt that's lying in the grass. This one looks like he's been raked by spur rowels." As he finished speaking, the large man grunted down from the saddle. To Frank he looked even larger on the ground. As he swept his coat back to stand with both hands on his hips Frank saw the badge. The big man said, "What's your name?"

"Frank Tennant."

"I'm Marshal Cord Bierk from Guadalupe. Villalobos said they beat hell out of you. For once in his life he told the gospel truth." Marshal Bierk paused, listening to the sound of men crunching gravel as they came around to the east side of the thicket. "Frank Tennant. You're the one George Medina hid out and patched up."

"Who told you that?" Tennant asked.

"Cruz Villalobos, the same man who sold you out to the Durans. He came foggin' it back to town to roust me out and tell me where you were and who had you." Marshal Bierk rummaged in a deep coat pocket, brought forth an empty brandy bottle, and grinned. "It wasn't too hard trackin' you until the moon left. After that it got a little harder until we found this bottle. Did you throw it down?"

"Yes." Frank turned his head slightly to watch the other men with carbines approach. He recognized Sam Smith by his coat and hat, stared at him briefly, then faced Bierk as he spoke again. "The one with the busted arm is Pete Duran. The dead one is . . ."

"I know who they are," Bierk said, returning the little bottle to his coat pocket. "I've known 'em off and on since they come around Guadalupe lookin' for you."

"Where is Ash Duran?"

"Around here someplace?"

"No. He left early last night heading for Guadalupe to get supplies."

The other riders stopped. One man tossed Frank his shirt and shook his head. "Mister, you look like you been kicked in the face by a mule, then run through a meat grinder."

Tennant was putting on the shirt when he replied. "Partner, that is just about how I feel." He saw Sam Smith glaring and was buttoning the shirt when he said, "You were goin' to shoot him. He's too worn out to run, he's got a busted arm, and he wasn't even armed."

Smith curled his lip. "Good thing for you, mister, that you missed."

Bierk cut in. "Sam, you boys load up the dead one. Tie him good. Then rig up another horse for the other one. If we're real lucky we just might see Ash Duran while we're headin' for home."

Frank sighed. He was thirsty, hungry, sore all over, and tired to the marrow in his bones. But there was something on his mind. "Marshal, if you find Ash he'll be carrying a pair of saddlebags with a lot of money in them. It belongs to me and . . ."

Bierk was turning to mount as he interrupted. "The way I heard it, you stole that money from a feller named Charley Burton, who's got quite a spread southwest of here down along the border."

Bierk looked down from the saddle while evening up his reins. They exchanged a long look. It was neither the time nor place for this particular discussion. As Bierk turned, Frank walked along beside him. They got around to the clearing where the other men already had Al lashed belly down and were helping Pete toward a saddled horse. Pete asked if anyone had whiskey. The man who had it, and who offered it, was Sam Smith. Pete evidently did not recognize him. He took the bottle, ignored Tennant's stare at Smith, the man who had tried to kill Pete and who was now giving him whiskey to help with his pain, swallowed three times, and returned the bottle with a gruff, "Thanks."

Smith went to his horse to stow the bottle, saw Frank staring at him, and said, "You need a drink too?"

Tennant shook his head and went after one of the canteens.

It was cool but the sun was climbing. Frank thought they

might make it back to Guadalupe before the heat arrived. He had been studying the sky, the horizon, the land on all sides, when a thick-chested man with a cud in his cheek and tolerant brown eyes came up on his left side, smiled, and said, "You lookin' for rain?"

Tennant studied the easy-going face. "No. The heat."

"Oh. It'll be along. We'd ought to be back to town before it turns really hot. I'm Bud Shilling, saddle an' harness maker in Guadalupe." Bud nodded his head without extending a hand.

Frank looked more closely at the man with gray above his ears. "Do you have a feller workin' for you?"

Bud was looking straight ahead when he nodded. "Yep. George Medina." He turned his head slowly. "Cord got him out of bed early this mornin' and locked him in the jailhouse."

Frank met the harness maker's gaze, read in it all he had to know, and said, "All he and his daughter did was take in a man they found half dead in their goat corral."

Bud did not argue. "Yeah. Trouble is, George knew the law wanted you. I was there in the shop several times when Cord Bierk come in to talk about you. George never opened his mouth." Bierk turned, leaned, spat amber, and straightened back around in the saddle. "Cord's goin' to ask you how much you paid Medina to hide you."

"Nothing," stated Frank. "Not a red cent."

Bud twisted to glance over his shoulder as he casually said, "Sure." Then he jutted his jaw. "See that feller back yonder named Smith, the one you was mad at? Well, Sam shot a lot of men in his time. Then he got hit, come down with an infection an' a fever." Bud straightened around looking at Tennant, almost grinning. "The Lord come to him, told him He wouldn't let Sam die if he'd mend his ways and help the Lord cleanse the land an' bring order to it."

Frank looked back at Sam Smith, who was riding beside Pete Duran with the whiskey bottle in his lap, earnestly talking. Pete looked pained at what he was hearing. As Frank came back around in the saddle, he caught Bud Shilling's hint of a grin and shook his head. "All right, him and the Lord are partners at saving souls. He's wasting his time back there with Pete Duran. But that's not what bothers me, Mister Shilling. He was going to kill Pete where Duran sat like a bird on a fence."

Bud's retort was short. "I didn't say I understand Sam, I just told you what he said one night when he got drunk. That was four years back. He's never been drunk since. I leave him alone—friendly an' all, but that's the end of it. You see the tall, skinny feller riding the rawboned sorrel horse— the man with the turkey neck?"

Frank looked back briefly, and nodded.

"Well, that's Will Perkins. He owns the saloon in town. He was a cattle rustler until he got caught and sent away, served his time, got out, bought a horse, and headed south. Told me one time he didn't figure to stop ridin' until he got so far that if someone asked him where he was from an' when he said Montana, they'd ask him where that was."

Frank Tennant had a vertical line between his eyes and an expression of wonder on his battered face as he gazed at the harness maker. "Looks like everyone in Guadalupe has something to hide."

Bud arose in his stirrups, resettled himself in the saddle and with a hard twinkle, said, "You asking about Cord Bierk?"

Frank shook his head. "No. You."

The hard look of dry amusement lingered. "Well now, Mister Tennant, seein' as how you robbed a man's strongbox, I expect we're all sort of birds of a feather, eh? Me? I robbed stages. Tried a bank once, figured to graduate into bigger things."

"How much did you get?"

The hard twinkle was still in place when Bud replied. "Five years hard labor an' a bullet through the leg."

Frank rode fifty yards in silence before twisting to look back again. Marshal Bierk, no longer wearing his coat, was leading Al Duran's horse. He still looked as broad as the rear end of a stud horse.

Bud interrupted his thoughts. "The marshal? Well now, he come from Texas. There's an old cowman around the country named Brent Campbell who knew the marshal down there. Only his name wasn't Bierk then, it was Berg. Carl Berg. He was a rangeman in Texas. He got into trouble. Mex border jumpers come up in the night, shootin' and hollerin' most likely drunk as lords. They would have run off the remuda of the outfit the marshal worked for, except that he outrun the other fellers, got into some rocks in a pass where the Mexicans had to go through, and shot out his carbine an' pistol, then reloaded and went down and finished the job. There was hell to pay. He headed west from Texas, met old Brent Campbell, who talked him into settlin' in Guadalupe, an' he's been here ever since."

Frank did not see distant dust because he was regarding the harness maker. "He's goin' to lock me up because he thinks I stole some money—him, a wanted man? All of you . . ."

"No. Now don't get upset, Mister Tennant. As far as we know, you did steal that money. But the man you stole it from—well—we've been hearin' about him for years. He peddles weapons to the Mexicans along with whiskey, then they come up over the line to raise hell. He buys looted gold from Mexican churches and sells stolen horses down in Mexico. But he's not in trouble, you are."

Frank looked back again, then frowned at Bud Shilling. "Fugitives. Every damned one of you."

Bud laughed. "Once, maybe. A long time back. But that's history now. We mind the law in Guadalupe, an' the marshal enforces it." Bud's eyes narrowed at Tennant. "I wish to hell some other Mex had looked after you. George Medina's the best man I ever had workin' in the shop with me." Bud's narrowed, appraising eyes did not waver. "I was saddlin' up gettin' ready to join the posse when a real nice an' very pretty girl come up." He paused until he saw understanding in Tennant's face, then he continued. "She begged me with tears in her eyes not to let anything bad happen to you."

Up ahead in the roadway, someone raised a loud call to announce the return of Marshal Bierk and his riders. People tumbled from stores and residences to watch them enter town.

CHAPTER 13

Turmoil in Guadalupe

GUADALUPE did not have a doctor, but Father Francis, the priest from the Mission, had been tending folks for many years, patching them, splinting broken limbs, dosing for fever and purging for various kinds of poison.

When Marshal Bierk and Frank Tennant were alone in the jailhouse office, the marshal went to the door, yelled to a loafer over in front of the general store, then closed the door and nodded his head in the direction of a hanging olla. Frank lifted it down and drank until sweat popped out all over him. Bierk watched from behind his untidy table, hat shoved far back. As Frank returned to the wall bench, Cord Bierk said, "The posse men'll tank up and eat, then we're goin' after Ash Duran. Do you have a notion which direction he might have taken?"

Frank told Bierk all he knew, which was that the eldest Duran had said he'd come to the spring after he got supplies in Guadalupe.

Bierk regarded Tennant for a long, silent moment before speaking. "Yeah. I watched for him, for some dust, anything that'd look like he was comin' back. There was some dust, but it was a Mex on his burro drivin' some milk goats." The marshal stood up as his roadway door opened, and a thick, squatty man in a dusty, brown cassock entered, black eyes taking in everything as he shoved the door closed at his back. He was carrying a little wooden box that had a rope handle.

Cord Bierk smiled. "Take your shirt off, Tennant." As Frank was obeying, the marshal exchanged a look with the priest and shrugged mighty shoulders without saying a word.

Father Francis was much older than he looked. His fleshy

face and neck, as well as coarse, black hair without a strand of gray in it, contributed to his appearing younger than his seventy years.

He pushed his face within inches of Frank's face and pursed his lips, raised a strong hand, and gently probed the swollen nose. Frank did not wince, but water started in his eyes. The priest turned to Marshal Bierk as though they were collaborators and Frank was a specimen. "It's not broken." Bierk sat down at his table, clasped big hands atop it, and watched the priest go to work.

The scratches required washing. They were not serious. Father Francis layered them with lanolin, told Frank to put his shirt back on and sit down. He then went to work on the discolored, puffy, torn face. As he worked he said, "What were you hit with?"

Frank fished in a trouser pocket and held up the massive golden crucifix. Both the older men stared. Father Francis gently touched the crucifix, then went back to work without a word. It was Marshal Bierk who asked who had hit Tennant in the face.

"Ash Duran. Right after they took me off the stagecoach."

Bierk nodded. "And the driver?"

"He had been paid to stop out there where they were waiting."

Bierk wrote a name on a scrap of paper, tossed down the pencil, and tossed his hat onto the seat of a nearby chair so he could vigorously scratch his head. Then he arose, hitched his holstered Colt into its proper position, and said, "Father, I'm in a sort of hurry."

The priest stepped back looking at Frank's face. "That's all I can do, Marshal. It will heal in time—the swelling will leave." He was putting the jar of lanolin grease back into his little box with the rope handle when he said with deliberate casualness, "I'd like to see Jorge Medina."

"Maybe tomorrow, Father. Right now I got to lock this one

up and round up my posse men. There's still one missing an' he's the most important one of them all."

Bierk herded the priest out, closed the roadway door, took down some keys on a copper ring, and took Tennant down into his cell room. He locked Frank into a strap-steel cage across from Medina. The older man was sitting slumped on a wall bunk and did not recognize Frank until after the lawman had departed, locking the cell-room door from the office.

Medina stared, slowly arose, and went to the front of his cell. "What happened to you? You look terrible."

Frank sat on his cot looking out across the little corridor. "The Durans caught me. A man named Villalobos told them how to catch me. They paid the son of a bitch fifty dollars. Then Villalobos rode back here, rousted out the marshal, and he tracked us down by moonlight. One of the Durans is dead. A rattler bit him. Pete, the other one . . . the last time I saw him the harness maker and the saloon owner were taking him somewhere. He has a broken arm. Unless they hang him I expect he'll show up in here with us."

"Where is your money?"

"The eldest Duran has it. That's where Marshal Bierk and his posse men are going now. To find him if they can."

There was much to discuss. They were still talking when Frank leaned back on the cot and simply went to sleep. By then it was early afternoon, and while the heat was driving people indoors throughout town, inside the thick-walled old mud jailhouse, it was still cool. The walls were three feet thick. At one time, many years before the *norteamericanos* won the Southwest from Mexico in a bitter war, this structure had been a powder magazine. At the height of South Desert summers, when nothing moved between noon and nine o'clock at night, Marshal Bierk's jailhouse never got above seventy degrees.

What awakened Tennant was the return of the squatty priest and a large, young blond man who accompanied Pete

Duran. They put Pete in the cell adjoining Medina's and left without more than a glance at the other prisoners. Pete's arm was slung in what appeared to be an old towel, which was looped around his neck. His face had been heavily salved. He ignored Medina and looked steadily at Frank Tennant without saying a word, then abruptly turned to lie out full length on his wall bunk. The mattress had been stuffed with what sounded like dry cornhusks as Duran tried to get comfortable.

Medina and Tennant exchanged a look and a shrug and went to their bunks. Frank's rest had helped, but now he was hungry enough to eat a bear, beginning in back if there was someone to hold its head.

Medina dozed. Pete Duran was motionless, staring at the ceiling. Frank studied his cell. It was one of those prefabricated cages made in a blacksmith shop and reassembled at the jailhouse. What light came in, did so from a long, very narrow, barred window in the rear wall of the cage. It was too narrow for a man to squeeze through and had steel bars set about six inches apart in the thick adobe wall. Otherwise, there was the bunk and a three-legged little stool. In the farthest corner was a lard bucket.

Frank eased back, stretched out, and closed his eyes. The hunger would have to wait; he was totally at the mercy of whoever supervised prisoners. He assumed that would be the big, hard-faced lawman, and he was God-only-knew-where, so the hunger would have to be borne.

He slept again, did not awaken until it was dark, and would not have awakened then except that George Medina was calling his name. "Frank? Frank! There is a commotion in the office."

Tennant swung his feet to the floor, winced, and stood up to approach the front of his cell. In the adjoining cage Pete Duran was snoring; in his line of work a man slept hard when he got the opportunity to sleep at all.

Medina was gripping the straps of his cage, straining to

hear. The difficulty appeared to be the massive oaken cell-room door; the voices were often loud, interrupting one another, but despite obvious agitation up there, what was being said did not penetrate coherently to the lower end of the cell room.

Frank looked across at Medina. "Maybe they caught the son of a bitch," he said. Medina shook his head. He did not think that was it, but he did not offer an opinion—he was instead concentrating on listening.

Eventually the noise diminished, then seemed to stop altogether, but that could have been an error; normal conversation from Marshal Bierk's office was not audible in the cell room at any time.

Tennant felt his face. Surprisingly, all of the fever was gone, and most of the swelling had atrophied. This held his interest after the noise had died away up yonder and George Medina had abandoned his effort to make out words. Frank asked Medina if he could see Frank's face well enough to notice any change. Medina tried, but since no one had lighted the hanging lamp in the corridor, and what little light came through the narrow, high windows was not enough, he had to shake his head. Then he smiled, showing white teeth in the gloom. "If it feels better, then you know why we put so much confidence in Father Francis."

The oaken door opened, light pushed the darkness into inaccessible corners as two people came toward the lower end of the room. One was Antonia. She was carrying a large basket. The other person was that big blond man who had been with the priest when they led Pete Duran to a cell. He was not armed; he did not have to be. He was easily six and a half feet tall with shoulders, arms, and legs as massive as the trunk of a seasoned oak tree.

Antonia stared at Frank, evidently speechless at his appearance. With better visibility, her father spoke from behind her. "You should have seen him earlier. Now, he looks very much better."

The big blond man was impatient. He took the basket from Antonia, yanked aside the gingham napkin, dug down, and brought forth the food, which he shoved at Medina first, then at Tennant. He looked in at Pete Duran, who was still making noises like a pig caught under a gate, then ignored him as Antonia turned her back on Frank and held her father's hand through the bars. He was eating with the other hand and looked calmly at her. "It will be all right," he said gently.

She blurted out words in a rush. "They killed Marshal Bierk."

Medina stopped chewing. Frank Tennant had been raising a chicken leg to his mouth. It remained in midair. Both men stared, first at the beautiful girl, whose features seemed frozen in their expression of horror, then at the big blond man, who raised his head. He had one hand in the basket, evidently to portion out more of whatever was in it.

Frank said, "Is it true?"

The large young man soberly nodded his head. "Yeah. He's lyin' on the office floor. They brought him in maybe an hour ago."

Medina finished chewing and swallowed. "Who? How did it happen?"

The blond man stopped fishing in the basket. "All I know is that the posse come back with the marshal face down over his horse an' Sam Smith the corralyard boss shot through the upper leg. Mister Shilling said it was an ambush."

Medina and Tennant exchanged a swift look. "An ambush by Ash Duran?"

The big young man answered shortly. "Naw. Maybe he was among them, no one knows, but it was more'n one man. Mister Shilling thinks there had to be at least six of them according to the gunfire."

Antonia took back her basket, divided the remaining food between Tennant and her father, then went closer to Frank's cage and offered cool fingers. He ran his hand down a trouser leg before touching her. She squeezed. He squeezed. She squeezed back and the blond man shuffled his feet impatiently. "You said you wanted to feed 'em. All right, you did it. Now I got work to do. Bein' temporary town marshal isn't anythin' I wanted to be, but I'm it, and there's a lot of activity around town tonight. Ma'am, come along now."

Frank stopped them both. "Wait. Where did it happen?"

"Hell, I don't know. Everyone was talkin' at once when the posse men came back," stated the blond man.

"Are they going to round up more men and go after them?"

The blond man looked exasperated. "Mister, all I can tell you is that right now Sam Smith's gettin' his leg patched up by the priest an' the others is over at the saloon. That's where I'm goin'. Ma'am, let's get out of here."

Antonia hesitated long enough to swiftly kiss her father, hesitate a moment or two longer, then raise on her tiptoes and pull Frank to her through the bars, and also kiss him. Then she hurried after the big blond man.

Medina was eating again. For him the shock had passed. He looked across the corridor, which was dark and gloomy again after the oaken door had been slammed. In a calmly rational tone he said, "Your uncle?"

Frank went to perch on his bunk with food in both hands. The idea had not occurred to him. Now, as he considered it, he remembered all the things the harness maker had told him about Cord Bierk and those other riders who had gone north with him to find Tennant and the Durans. He said, "Maybe. But from what I know about this country, Jorge, there are outlaws, or at least fugitives just about everywhere. And the stories Antonia told me of Mex border jumpers . . . Hell, it could have been any of them."

Medina finished a chicken back and tossed it into the lard bucket behind him. As he wiped his hands on a red bandanna he said, "Except for one thing. How did they know the posse was coming? In the dark, late at night? To make an ambush you have to know someone is coming toward the place where you are waiting. In this case how could they have known?"

Frank turned to peer through the gloom. "Villalobos again?"

Medina shrugged and went back to his bunk to sit down without answering.

CHAPTER 14

A Three-quarter Moon

THE second time the big blond who was the acting town marshal came down into the cell room, he had Bud Shilling with him. George Medina nodded without smiling, until the man he had worked for so long grinned, reached through, and roughly rapped Medina on the shoulder. Medina smiled. "You smell of whiskey," he said. Shilling's grin remained in place. "Those of us who came back earned it, George."

"What happened?"

Shilling turned toward Frank Tennant, a speculative look replacing his grin. He did indeed smell of whiskey; in a small, thick-walled room where ventilation was poor, the smell was particularly noticeable.

The blond man leaned on Duran's cell, looking in and shaking his head. "If he wasn't snorin' I'd say he was dead. How can a man sleep half the day away and part of the night?"

The other three men ignored this. Shilling spoke slowly. "It was Bierk's idea. Sam and me thought it was crazy. Cord wanted to ride in the direction of that spring again. He said sure as hell Ash Duran was over there someplace. Maybe prowlin' around tryin' to figure out what happened to Tennant and his brothers.

"Sam said no man with thirty thousand greenbacks in his saddlebags would be lookin' for his brothers or anyone else—he'd be hightailin' it out of the country as fast as he could. Maybe south toward the border. Maybe southwest toward the California trace." Shilling paused to glance at Frank Tennant before resuming.

"You want to know why I'm here right now?" Before Frank

113

could answer, the harness maker reverted to his former recitation. He did not seem drunk, but Frank surmised he'd had enough to create some minor problems with his ability to concentrate.

"We'll get to that," Shilling said. "Anyway, when we was maybe a fair distance south and east of that damned spring, Cord said we'd ought to spread out. We could cover more ground that way. He wouldn't listen to any of us. George, you know how he was. Once Cord Bierk got an idea in his head you couldn't budge it with dynamite.

"So we fanned out. It wasn't real dark. There was a moon." Shilling paused, staring at the stone floor. "It happened so goddamned fast. We'd been saddlebackin' since before dawn. I don't know about the others, but I was havin' a hell of a time stayin' awake.

"There wasn't any warning. Just gunfire. Muzzleblast as red as fire ahead of us along a front of maybe a hundred yards. Maybe more. We'd rode right into 'em.

"I heard someone cry out as I was divin' to the ground. Didn't have time to grab my carbine. I'm here to tell you I was wide awake. We fired back, kept it up for a long time until it dawned on me no one was shootin' back an' I yelled for the other fellers to stop.

"We lay there listening for a long time, maybe fifteen minutes, then Sam Smith began to swear. It didn't draw any gunfire. Hell, they was gone.

"We found Sam bleedin' like a stuck hog, tied his wound off, and went lookin' for the marshal. It must have been him that let go that first yelp. He was lyin' on his side like he was asleep, with a hole in his chest an inch or two away from his heart. I don't think he died instantly, but he sure as hell didn't have to wait long."

Frank was holding the straps of his cell. "Which way did they run?"

Shilling pulled out a handkerchief and mopped at his face before replying. "Don't know. By the time we got organized even the damned moon was gone. Behind a cloud for all we knew. Anyway, we had casualties." Shilling's eyes shifted. "No one really wanted to mount up and go lookin' for those bastards. I'll tell you for a fact there was at least half a dozen of them." He punched the handkerchief into a rear pocket and gazed at Frank Tennant. "We been talkin' over at Will's place. How the hell they knew we was out there was one thing. Another thing was that little bastard Villalobos. One thing led to another. We went down to Mex town lookin' for him. He wasn't there. An old man who was scairt peeless told us Villalobos left on his black horse about dusk, which would have been close to the time we was gettin' organized to ride. The old man said he went southwest like the devil was behind him." Shilling paused again, still looking steadily at Frank Tennant. "Will Perkins came up with an idea. Him and Cord was pretty good friends. They'd discussed Duran and that money. Bierk said he wouldn't bet a plugged centavo that the feller it was stolen from wouldn't come up here lookin' for the Durans and his money."

Frank was beginning to understand what all this talk was leading up to. To forestall more talk he said, "Charles Burton?" When the harness maker nodded, Frank glanced over his shoulder. Medina was leaning on the front of his cell, looking straight at Frank, and smiling.

"Yeah," Shilling replied. "Burton. Someone said you was related to him. They said they'd heard you claimed that money was yours, not Burton's."

The big blond man was shifting his feet, clearly wearying of this. Pete Duran's snoring had changed pitch; it sounded more shallow now, less moist and bubbly, but it did not stop.

Shilling continued to unwaveringly regard Tennant. "I'll tell you something, though. If you agree to ride with us, act as guide, there's some fellers who'll shoot you in the back the minute they figure you're guidin' us wrong, maybe into another ambush."

Frank considered the blond man. He was staring straight

at Frank. He shifted slightly and met George Medina's gaze. Not a word passed between them, but Medina's expression hinted at doubts about the wisdom of Frank leading the Guadalupe posse men.

Shilling broke the hush. "You know the country down along the border where Burton hangs out?"

Frank knew it, but he did not say how: that he had worked for Charles Burton. "Yes, I know it."

"You willin' to ride with us? The whole town wants to settle up for what happened to Bierk and Sam Smith."

Medina spoke dryly. "And get shot in the back? You've been drinking, Bud."

Shilling looked around. "You know me better'n that, George. You've never seen me drunk in your life."

"There will be others," Medina stated quietly. He shifted his attention. "Let them do it without you, Frank. What do you owe them? You're in their jail, aren't you? No matter what you tell them on a stack of Bibles, they won't believe you."

Shilling's eyes flashed fire. He was by nature an easygoing, amiable, even garrulous individual, but like everyone else he had limits. "What are you tryin' to do?" he demanded of his employee.

"Save his life. Why should he help you, Bud?"

Shilling's angry expression did not fade. "If he wants to get out of this cell, he'd ought to help us."

Medina shrugged. "A cell is better than a grave."

Shilling glared at Medina, then faced back in Tennant's direction, still angry. "It's up to you. All I told 'em was that I'd talk to you about it."

During the exchange between Medina and the harness maker, Frank had been thinking. Now, he said, "Give me guns, and you ride beside me. I'll show you how to get down there. I'll even show you how to find Burton if I can, but if Ash Duran is with him and he still has my money in those saddlebags, I want it handed over—if we're successful. If we aren't, I want your word that no matter who says otherwise, you'll cover my back and let me ride away."

The blond man was no longer bored. George Medina waited until Frank had stated his terms, then turned toward his bunk, wagging his head.

Shilling stepped aside for the blond man to unlock the door. He was silent and expressionless as Tennant stepped past and started up the corridor behind Bud Shilling.

While Shilling and the acting town marshal were fitting Frank out with weapons in the office, Pete Duran finally coughed, cleared his pipes, opened his eyes, and raised up enough to see Medina. He eyed him for a moment, then said, "Anythin' goin' on?"

Medina turned slightly, then turned away as he replied. "No. Not a thing."

"When do we eat?"

"I don't know. Go back to sleep."

Duran grunted, rolled up onto his side, and did exactly that.

There was noise in the roadway that attracted Shilling to the office doorway. He looked out, stepped back, and addressed the blond man. "You comin' along, Max?"

The blond man was helping Tennant fill his depleted belt loops when he replied. "No, don't think I'd better, Mister Shilling. Someone's got to hang back an' mind the town."

Bud jerked his head at Frank Tennant, held the door for him to pass through first, then closed the door and eyed the lighted area down in front of the livery barn where men and saddle animals seemed to be mingling in confusion. He nudged Frank.

As they were walking, Frank hoisted the booted Winchester over his shoulder and considered his companion. Shilling had been friendly and affable on the ride back from the spring, but that was all Frank knew about him. He knew even less of the others, some of whom he had never seen before.

But he recognized smooth-faced Will Perkins the saloonman, who had at one time in his life been a cattle thief.

Shilling introduced him to Kent Duncan the liveryman, who was an overweight man with a lean face and a good smile. As Frank and Shilling walked toward the animal, which had been rigged out for Tennant, Bud leaned and said, "Used to be a highwayman. One of the best, so I've heard. Never got caught."

Tennant looked over his shoulder. The congenial liveryman was busy among the horses. There were six riders including the liveryman. They were armed to the gills, and while Frank was certain they had all been drinking, right now they were all business. Must have been the cooling night air.

Frank's animal was tall and rangy with a rear end that came off like an olive, thick, coarse legs, big feet, and a wide, deep chest. He was a peculiar color, somewhere between a *grulla* and sorrel, sort of soiled looking. He had a big head and little pig-eyes. As Frank stood eyeing him, the liveryman came up and said, "Yeah, I know. I've seen better-lookin' animals too. But let me tell you something, amigo. That horse's got more bottom than any horse around. He can lope a hole in the daylight, stop, take down a big breath, and do it all over again." Duncan gave Frank a light rap on the back and walked away.

They left town with a few straggling onlookers watching. Guadalupe seemed to have retired long ago. At least there were few lights showing. The brightest brilliance came from over the spindle doors and through the roadway windows of Perkins's saloon.

They walked their horses. Bud came up to Frank to gesture and say, "It's your foray, partner," and smiled. Frank stood in his stirrups and looked back. The other posse men were looking at him, and none of them were smiling. Frank eased down.

Cool night air felt good on his face. There was still discoloration, but most of the swelling was gone, and the discoloration was only slightly darker than his normal look. In the night it was scarcely noticeable.

He did not take a particular direction except to ride mostly southward. The moon was high. It was also fuller than it had been a couple of nights ago. He looked at the harness maker. "Some of you fellers ought to feel right at home." To clarify his meaning he tipped his head upward. Bud understood. Without smiling he said, "How old are you?"

"Twenty-nine. Unless this is July, then I'm thirty."

"It's May, an' I'm fifty-two. Bein' older don't guarantee anythin' except that you're a mite slower rollin' out in the morning, but right now I figure I'm wiser'n you, so I'll pass along a little advice. What I told you on the ride to town from the spring about these gents—I wouldn't keep harping on it if I was you."

Frank made one comment, then abided by Shilling's advice. He said, "The moon's three-quarters full. That's what they called a nightrider's moon when I was growing up."

Bud fished for his tobacco, acting as though he hadn't heard. An hour farther along, he asked if Frank knew where he was going. The answer he got was in the nature of an explanation. It was accompanied by a sweeping gesture from Tennant's right arm.

"If it was Burton, I can tell you from experience he's a very direct man. He'll be making tracks in a beeline for home. I can also tell you after what he did tonight, he's not going to just lope along. He's as crooked as a dog's hind leg and as leery as a wolf. He'll have a rider or two on his back trail a mile or so, waiting for pursuit. So, we're not goin' to chase after him. We're goin' to angle toward his place but from down closer to the border. When he gets down there, why then we'll turn due east."

Bud nodded. "How long'll it take?"

Frank looked up again before answering. "We'll be ridin' east before sunrise."

Shilling scowled. "From what I've heard, Burton's got sentinels out in all directions. In broad daylight . . ."

"We're not goin' to lock horns with him in daylight, Mister Shilling. We're goin' to hole up somewhere, make damned sure the animals are plumb rested before evening, then we're goin' on in."

Bud chewed, rode in silence for a while, then without another word to Frank, hauled back, waited until Perkins and a couple of the other older riders came up, and told them what Tennant had said.

They listened in solemn silence, then nodded. As Shilling had said, or had at least implied, these were men with experience at riding toward trouble under a two-thirds full moon. Kent Duncan rolled a smoke with looped reins, lit up inside his hat, picked up the reins, and trickled smoke as he gazed ahead through narrowed eyes at Tennant's back. "He got away with thirty thousand dollars, Bud?" Shilling nodded. "Well, seems a mite young to me, but I can't fault his success."

There was a low murmur of approval. Only one man questioned Frank's knowledge of the country he was leading them to. Shilling's answer to that silenced him. "He went down there alone, got past all Burton's wolves, raided his strongbox, and came within an ace of getting clean away. He couldn't have done it, Albert, unless he damned well knew the country."

Duncan removed his quirley to comment. "And the men he was goin' up against don't seem to have been greenhorns."

Nothing more was said.

When Frank raised his arm and brought it down—at the same time boosting the big, ugly rawboned horse over into an easy, mile-eating lope—the others followed his example.

CHAPTER 15

The Arroyo

BY the time they were riding due east, they were less than five or six miles from the border and dawn was coming.

Finding a place to loaf the daylight hours away was not a problem. There was underbrush and even a few fields of horse-high big old, ugly, dark rocks, but what Frank was aiming for was water, so he put a man out front to scout and kept riding. Bud was beginning to worry about the time the sun arrived. He and the others were watching Frank like a hawk but said nothing.

He led them down a gradual wide slope until the landform on both sides was higher than they were. He did not look back until the broad arroyo made a big swooping northward turn with some kind of trees up ahead with tight, mottled bark and flattened tops.

The animals smelled the water.

Where Frank dismounted, there was sign of cattle having been down here recently; the horn flies had not all departed.

The horsemen swung off, looking around. Where they were standing, the gully was about a hundred yards wide, with sloping, high walls where bunchgrass grew but no underbrush. The water had been developed into a long pool with rocked-up places to keep it from flowing freely until it overflowed the rockwork.

Kent Duncan finished hobbling his horse first and strolled over, pulling off his gloves. He smiled at Frank. "No mistake," he opined, "you do know this country. I been down on the border with freight wagons a hunnert times, and so help me, I never saw this place before."

When Frank replied, the other men were listening. "Bur-

121

ton's riders use it to hold cattle until dark before delivering them south of the border." He was smiling at Duncan but looking around for Will Perkins the former rustler as he explained. Perkins was tying his coat behind the saddle with his back to the others. He had already made his private appraisal of this place.

They went under one of those flat-topped trees into shade. Over there Frank mentioned sentries. From appearances and the faint rank smell, he knew those cattle who had left a few horn flies behind had been down here no more than twenty-four hours earlier.

He did not believe Burton's riders would bring another herd down here very soon. Nevertheless, as he told the men, they were in Charles Burton's country. He had a number of men working for him, and all they would need would be for some rider to pass along on the desert above and see them down here.

Two of the posse men turned to start the climb to higher ground. They took Winchesters with them.

The remaining men got comfortable in shade even though it was still cool, dug out jerky, and watched as Frank used a dead twig to give them an idea of where they were, then to sketch what was ahead. "We're a little more'n halfway. Here— this is a town called Slaughterville, but it's farther east. We won't have any reason to go there." He scratched more lines before continuing. "This is Burton's place. These are corrals and buildings."

A man made a low whistle. "Big, ain't it?"

Frank looked up. "The yard's about fifteen acres. There are always cattle and horses in the corrals. Wagons come an' go just about every day." He paused, then painstakingly drew more lines. "This is Burton's house."

Bud Shilling scowled. "Are those smaller squares where his riders live?"

"Yeah, and teamsters, and men like the Duran brothers

who police both sides of the border to make damned sure nothing goes wrong."

Bud still scowled. "Are we goin' to his house, for Cris'sake? It's right smack-dab in the middle of where all his hands live."

Frank tossed the twig away and looked steadily at the harness maker. "There's not enough of us to ride in shooting. I may have to go to the main house but you fellers don't. I want my money back. Otherwise, from this canyon we'll go slightly upcountry after dark. There's some old crumbling adobe shacks. They belonged to Mex contraband runners years ago, before Charley Burton ran them off. Those shacks are on both sides of the trail used for takin' livestock into the yard, and out."

Kent Duncan squinted his eyes. "Ambush?" he asked quietly, and Tennant nodded his head.

Will Perkins, Bud Shilling, and Kent Duncan settled back in the shade. Frank spoke to the liveryman. "Mister Duncan, do you still have a big, leggy horse branded FT on the left shoulder?"

Duncan was building a smoke and did not look up as he replied. "Well, yes, I got him in the public corrals. He goes up for auction for his keep directly." Duncan lit up, blew smoke, and eyed Tennant. "Your horse?"

"Yes."

Duncan was not surprised. "Villalobos found him out in Dominguez Canyon."

"How much you got against him?" Frank asked, and the liveryman considered droopy ash on his cigarette as he replied. "Let's see how this mess comes out, then we'll talk about that. Cord Bierk was a friend of mine. If you can get us into position to settle up for him, why I suppose I wouldn't have much against your horse at all."

Bud Shilling looked pleased. He rolled his eyes and said, "Mister Tennant, a man could do a lot worse than settle around Guadalupe. There's some sly ones around, but mostly folks are decent enough."

Perkins removed his hat to mop sweat off a nearly hairless pate. His look at the harness maker showed annoyance, but he kept silent.

They rested. Frank slept for a while, until the two sentries returned, then he and the saloonman picked up Winchesters and went up above the arroyo to replace them.

Now, there was heat. Will Perkins pointed with his carbine barrel where there was pale shade on the lee side of a dense thicket and led the way. From this place they could see in three directions. Where the thicket prevented visibility in the fourth direction, they could stand up occasionally and look over it.

Perkins got comfortable. "I own the saloon," he said. "I heard talk about you bein' related to this Charley Burton feller."

"My uncle," stated Frank, scuffing aside dirt before sitting down.

"You don't like him?"

Frank was seated when he replied. "Got reason, Mister Perkins."

"Call me Will."

Frank told him about his uncle killing his mother while Frank had been away buying cattle. Perkins mopped his bald head again and reset his hat before speaking. "I come from Missouri, Frank. Between there and this here country, I rode with some pretty ornery fellers. But so help me, if what you just told me is true, why those friends of mine was pure as driven snow next to Burton. You want him or your money?"

"I want both."

"All right. I'll help you get 'im, an' if you fail, I'll do it. The money, well, you'll have to take most of the risks there. Us fellers from Guadalupe didn't come here for money. We want to settle up for Cord and Sam."

A pair of buzzards, fully mature with wide wingspans, soared over, then lazily wheeled to make a lower sweep.

Will tipped his head and watched them. As they widened their sweep to take in the deep arroyo and the men and horses down there, he said, "What's this Burton feller look like?"

Frank gave the description and Perkins stopped watching the buzzards, which were now going farther south on warm air until they were specks. "Just so's I'll know him when I see him," he murmured, and yawned, rubbed his eyes to stay awake, and did as Tennant was doing, ran a slow, narrow-eyed look out and around where the land was beginning to shimmer.

It was empty. There was no movement, which was what both men were watching for. But that was in three directions, north, south, and west. Behind them eastward there was dust at a considerable distance as the sentinels drowsed, fighting to remain awake, lulled by heat and boredom. Will Perkins sighed and cleared his throat. It was the only sound. Its effect was to make his companion's head come up, his eyes to pop wide open.

Perkins had his knees drawn up, the Winchester between them, his left hand lightly holding the gun. He was watching a gila monster. When the fat, ugly thing came close enough, Perkins spat at it. The lizard was motionless for a long while. It knew the men were there, backs to its thicket, but it could not establish the difference between sitting human forms and the thick background of underbrush. Neither man moved. The gila monster was the only thing to watch.

Its bite was poisonous, but rangemen, and even people who lived in towns and villages, were not especially fearful. For one thing, gila monsters with their distinctive colors, their short legs, and dim minds, were not fast at either striking or attacking.

When Will scuffed dirt at it, it did not even hiss. When Perkins slowly grasped his carbine in both hands and leaned forward to nudge the creature, it gave a little start and went scurrying northward, waddling from side to side in what was, to gila monsters, great haste.

The saloonman raised his hat to mop off sweat, lowered the hat, and turned. Frank Tennant was sitting very straight, head slightly to one side. Without a word he unwound up off the ground and stepped past Perkins toward the upper end of their thicket. Perkins grunted upright.

Frank stood motionless and silent for a long while. When the older man came up, he stepped to Tennant's left, and noisly sucked in his breath.

Horsemen!

Frank jerked his head. They both faded back behind the thicket. Tennant said, "Go on back. Warn the others. The way they're riding I'd say they could pass north of us half a mile or so. Tell 'em to get the horses hid, take their carbines and get out of sight down there, watching this rim."

Perkins turned southward without a word. Just before he started downward, he faced around. "If they come down into the arroyo . . ."

Frank Tennant was down on one knee shadowed by the thicket when he replied. "Then we got serious trouble. Looks like five or six of 'em. Go on."

The saloonman disappeared, leaving Frank leaning on his carbine watching the riders. They did not ride like men in a hurry. They rode bunched up the way horsemen do when they are talking back and forth. This is what made it difficult for Frank to be sure of their numbers. This, and the distance. They looked to be about a mile and a half eastward, far enough for the heat haze, which shimmered like jelly, to obscure details.

They had come from the east. Frank guessed they had left Burton's yard right after breakfast, maybe earlier. They were riding to parallel the canyon, but of course that could change at any time.

Two were Mexicans, recognizable by their huge hats. The

others were gringos. Frank had at one time known just about every one of his uncle's employees, but in the business Charley Burton was engaged in, hirelings came and went with probably much more frequency than in other lines of work.

Frank's throat was dry. Neither he nor Will had brought a canteen up here with them. Sweat was running beneath his shirt. Twice, before the little band of unsuspecting riders got close enough for details to be visible, he dried both palms down the sides of his britches legs.

He was mystified by the purpose for those men to be out here if they were not heading for the arroyo, which they did not seem to be interested in. They did not alter course as they would have done if the canyon had been their destination.

He heard their voices indistinctly until one of them laughed. He knew that laugh. It belonged to a dark, heavyset Mexican named Rosario Valdez. Frank Tennant and Valdez had worked together many times.

Valdez was the best man with a reata or lass-rope Frank had ever seen. He could put sixty feet of braided rawhide through the air with unfailing accuracy. He was one of Charles Burton's oldest employees. He was also a good-natured, shrewd, tough, and durable individual without a shred of discernment. He had told Frank several times that to someone who had grown up in a land where men shot one another for their boots, or sometimes for no reason at all except that they were handy targets, no one lived to maturity believing there was any such thing as either right or wrong. There was only survival.

They had been close, had shared bottles of *pulque*, jokes, and risks. As Frank eased back with infinite slowness until he was completely mottled by underbrush and its shadows, he studied the others. The second *vaquero* was a stranger to him. He was young, rode with a relaxed, supple body, as only people did who had learned to ride only a short while after they had learned to walk, and had his big sorrel colt in a hackamore.

Those two, Rosario Valdez and the younger Mexican, partially concealed the rider on their right. The other three men, the gringos, were unknown to Frank, but he squinted at them hard to get some idea of their character and capabilities. The best he could do at that distance with hazy visibility was to decide they were the only kind of men his uncle hired: seasoned, hard, deadly individuals.

The pair of Mexicans abruptly broke away from the others to lope ahead. Out where they slackened to a walk, both men rode, leaning slightly from their saddles. They were looking for tracks.

Frank let go a long breath. He should have expected it. His uncle had wasted no time after returning safely to his yard. He had sent these riders out to scout for the tracks of pursuers. He had probably sent other riders out farther northward for the same purpose.

Frank turned back from watching the scouts and saw the rider who had been hidden by the *vaqueros*.

It was Ash Duran!

He backed deeper into the thicket, had to push sweat off his forehead before it got into his eyes, and did not take his eyes off Duran until the riders were a fair distance westward, far enough to preclude much chance of them turning southward to the arroyo.

He slid down the grassy bank and went swiftly back to the area of the spring, where the men who had watched his approach came out of hiding.

He drank deeply at the spring, filled his hat with water, and upended it over his head, then he turned to tell the others what he had seen and what he knew Burton's men were doing, and that brought up everyone's attention. Kent Duncan said, "Hell, if they go far enough, they're goin' to come across our sign. Frank, they can track us right down into this canyon."

Bud Shilling, who usually smiled a lot, was not doing it now. He was thinking. Eventually he said, "Let me tell you boys a secret of mine—the difference between success and failure when you're about to have someone force your back to the wall, is to figure ahead."

Since this enigmatic remark meant nothing to the others, they scowled. Bud finally smiled. "Now then, we know they're out yonder, an' we know what they're doin' out yonder, an' we know sooner or later they'll find our sign, turn back, and follow it right down here." The smile widened.

A growly voice said, "Yeah. Catch us down in here. Bud, this damned canyon's a regular coffin."

Shilling's smile was crafty. "Maybe it is for a fact. But if we figure things, it won't be our coffin." He twisted to look back in the direction they had ridden to get here and gestured. "Them sidehills got grass an' no underbrush. But in the middle of the draw there's so much cover hell couldn't hold it all." He faced them. "They're comin' to look for us. Well, we been figurin' and we're not goin' to be this far into the arroyo. Our tracks will be but we won't. We'll be up near the top-out where we started down in here, an' we'll be hid somewhere. I expect they'll get leery about comin' down in here after us. Maybe they'll split up an' ride the rims lookin' for someone to shoot at from up there.

"But we're goin' to be 'way back there. Up as close as we can get to the upper slope. You understand?"

They understood. Frank could not resist making a dry comment. "Bud, a man's got to have a real devious mind to think like you do."

Shilling was not the least offended. He smiled and winked. "Is that what it is? I always figured it was just plain common sense. Don't sit and wait. Go right up to whoever is after you and blow up in their face." His smile wavered. "Tell you what I think though—maybe they wouldn't be able to hear shooting back at Burton's yard, but maybe there is other riders out who would hear it. Let's see if we can't catch these fellers without any shooting. Sure make things easier if we could."

It was not a complicated plan, and because they had plenty of time to talk about it, because at the rate Burton's riders had been going west they would not find the tracks until the middle of the afternoon, they trooped back to the shade.

CHAPTER 16

A Time for Nerves

THERE had been ugly, large, scabrous rocks a half mile or so westward where the land had begun to tip downward. The decision was to go back up there on foot, staying to the sidehills so there would be no boot tracks showing at the approach to the arroyo, and find places of concealment up there.

Frank listened to these men, former outlaws to a man, with candid interest. They were discussing the ambush as though setting ambushes was a specialized game to them. Frank saw Bud Shilling watching him with a twinkle in his eyes. Frank wagged his head slightly and Bud's smile came up, but he said nothing.

When they were ready to leave the depth of the arroyo, where the flourishing undergrowth and trees were spring-water fed, each man had tied his horse out of sight and joined the others with a saddle gun as well as a belt gun.

Will Perkins came over to Tennant wearing a quizzical expression. "You got doubts?" he asked.

Frank shook his head, ruefully smiling. "No. It's just that I never sat in on anything like this, Will."

Perkins nodded. "Well, now you have. I guess it don't happen to everyone." He looked around where the men were coming together and looked back, while hoisting his carbine to his shoulder, holding it by the barrel. "It always goes about like this, whether you're part of a rustling gang or a band of horse thieves. There's got to be a plan."

Frank could understand that. He said, "I reckon so. But you'n Bud an' the others enjoyed it, Will."

Perkins's features came close to a smile. "It's a challenge. Plannin' sort of gets your blood to runnin'. Come along."

It was a long walk. On horseback it had not seemed as long. There was very little conversation. Kent Duncan was beside Frank, pushing his way through hard brush and soft creepers, when he said, "Sometimes a man wonders about how things work out. If we had Sam Smith along there'd be shootin' sure as hell."

Frank mentally agreed but said nothing. Bud and Will were leading, and their main consideration was to either hide tracks or leave them in places where a mounted man would not want to ride his horse unless he had to.

They reached the upper slope of the arroyo where there was less cover, none at all on the sides of the canyon, and here the men split, half making their way midway up the east sidehill, half climbing to the midpoint of the opposite slope. Tracks would be visible up there, but the gamble was that Burton's riders would not angle along the sidehills. It was a risk but, as Tennant told himself, there had to be risks—at least this one was stacked in their favor.

The air was hotter up here, visibility was not as limited, and by the time they were out of the canyon heading for some of those jumbles of dark, ancient rocks—even though the sun was reddening as it slanted lower down the western sky and for the most part was in their faces—it was possible to see for very great distances. It was also possible to notice that there was nothing out there. Not even any dust.

Frank was with Kent Duncan and a man named Albert Springer. Springer was a scarecrow of a man. Tall, skinny as a beanpole, with a deeply lined, weathered-dark face and perpetually narrowed eyes that seemed to miss nothing. Frank's impression was one of extreme wariness, even furtiveness. Bud had told him nothing about Albert, so Frank's assessment of the man had to be based upon his impression, plus his colored judgment of every man he was with.

They found an adequate place of concealment, which

Duncan said was too far from the entrance to the arroyo, so they went back to a lower scattering of stones where they could not stand up without being exposed, but which was close enough for them to be able to see their own earlier tracks. The sun did not beat on their backs, but it was in their faces when they raised up to look across where the other men were leaning in rock shade, watching the land where they expected to eventually see horsemen. Now and then one of them would casually twist to look across toward the rocks where Frank and his companions were.

Kent raised his hat to mop sweat. "Should have brought a canteen," he said.

Neither Frank nor Albert Springer commented on that.

Frank leaned his Winchester against a rock and tipped his hat down. That damned sun was going to be a problem unless Burton's riders did not appear until after it had set.

He rolled slightly to look at the man closest to him, Albert Springer. The lean, older man met his gaze without a word until Frank said, "Sure as hell must be an easier way to serve the Lord."

Springer grinned. "Most likely there is. Be a monk. Then you'd get bored to death instead of maybe shot to death."

Kent Duncan spoke up. "Albert, you always been such a cheerful cuss." He paused, twisted to look squarely at the thin man, and spoke again. "You ever sat out like this before?"

Springer squinted westward before answering, and even then he did not meet the liveryman's gaze. "Yep. Matter of fact I have."

Kent was encouraged by the answer. "Hidin' among the trees until a stagecoach come along, maybe?"

Springer continued to look westward. "You know, Kent, when I first came to the Guadalupe country, I was lookin' for someone."

"Did you find him?"

Albert settled against his rock to get more comfortable. "I

think so. You. The description fit to a T, except that you was a respectable businessman." Albert smiled at the liveryman. "Highwayman who got away with a crate of new greenbacks bein' sent down to Albuquerque from the Denver mint."

Kent also got more comfortable. He took a little time to peek over the top of his rock, not looking for riders or their dust, but to watch the men across the canyon. As long as they stood casually watching, Kent would not worry. He said, "How long you been tendin' bar for Will Perkins?"

"Four years."

"In that length of time we've talked a hundred times."

The weathered man nodded his head. "Sure have."

"You never said anythin' or made a move."

"It used to be deputy U.S. marshals could ride in, find their man, bypass the local law, and whisk him back to Denver. Times change, Kent. So do the rules. Commencing about six years back the law said a marshal had to have good enough proof to stand up in court."

Duncan faced the lean man. "You didn't?"

"Nope."

"You still lookin' for it?"

"Nope. I quit years ago and settled at Guadalupe. Too damned many laws and all. They tie a man's hands. You know something, Kent? I couldn't even walk up an' throw down on you. And I sure as hell couldn't have taken you back to Denver without havin' the cooperation of the local lawman, an' by gawd I had to get extradition papers from the governor of the damned territory."

Kent heaved a mighty sigh and wagged his head. "It's a damned shame what you boys got to go through."

They regarded each other for a moment, then laughed. Frank, who had been intrigued for a while, then definitely uneasy, laughed with them, but his laughter was prompted by relief.

Someone over across the canyon was waving his hat. Moments later, there was no one visible over there. Frank's heart thudded briefly when Albert Springer raised a bony arm. There was a faintly discernible dust banner coming from the west.

Albert calmly said, "Well, well, well. Now that's a nice sight, isn't it? I was beginnin' to get awful tired of this damned hard ground. You still thirsty, Kent?"

Duncan nodded. "You remindin' me don't help."

Springer's square, worn teeth showed in a hard grin, but he was watching the dust and said nothing more.

Frank caught some of the tough composure of his companions. He watched the dust too, and when the horsemen were near enough to be seen even though they were still a long way off, he told his friends about Rosario Valdez. He also told them about being struck in the face by Ash Duran. They knew some of what had transpired earlier but not the details. When they asked he told them.

Springer asked about the big golden crucifix, and Frank dug it out of his trouser pocket for the former deputy marshal to examine. Springer pursed his lips in a silent whistle and hefted the rosary. "Solid gold. This thing must be worth a lot of money." He handed it to Kent Duncan. "How much would you say it weighs?"

Duncan put his back to his rock and considered the rosary very closely, then passed it back to Frank without answering Springer's question. He said, "It belongs around your neck, not in your pocket."

Frank dutifully removed his old hat in order to do as the liveryman said. As he was settling his hat again, lower in front, Al Springer squirmed around, watched the approaching riders, then pulled out a blue bandanna and wrapped it around the old gray barrel of his carbine. Without commenting, both his companions did the same, although Frank thought there would be no sunlight to reflect off metal by the time Burton's riders got to the mouth of the wide arroyo.

Across the way the only sign of life was a mile or so

westward. Closer, in the rough black rocks where the other posse men were waiting, there was not a sign of humanity.

Springer softly said, "If this goes sour we still got 'em where the hair's short. They're goin' to be between two fires, and lower'n both. I like this kind of a bushwhack."

Frank saw Kent look at the lean man, then turn aside. Frank felt the same way. There was no valid reason to suspect Albert Springer was another Sam Smith, someone who shot first and looked afterward, but just now he certainly had sounded like one.

Down in the wide arroyo, several hundred yards north-ward, a horse whinnied. Frank leaned a little to look down there. He wasn't conscious of his nerves being on edge, but they were. The horse did not make another call. Frank got lower down against his rock as he said, "Damned animal."

Springer contradicted him. "Naw. If he'll do that when those gents get up to the beginning of the downward slope, maybe they'll think we're down there with our animals and ride right on down through."

Springer put a skeptical smile on Frank. "You never sat in on one of these dry gulches did you?"

Frank reddened slightly and shook his head.

"It's sort of like playin' checkers. We move, they move, an' someone makes a mistake an' you jump his man." Springer looked around in the liveryman's direction. "Is that about right?"

Duncan was watching the distant riders through eyes squeezed nearly closed as he replied. "Close enough."

For a moment Springer continued to look at the liveryman, then he too settled forward to watch the dust. Now, what had earlier appeared as riders down close to ant-size, looked different. They were still not close, but it was possible to make out two large Mexican sombreros among the smaller hats.

For Frank it was possible to recognize Rosario Valdez by his thick width.

Across the way, about a hundred yards west of the trail of shod-horse marks that led down into the arroyo, there was no sign of men in the rocks with weapons. But they were there. Frank could almost visualize Bud Shilling's triumphant smile. This had been his idea and right now it appeared to have a good chance of succeeding.

Frank had never seriously thought that it might not. As long as his uncle's hard riders followed the tracks, they were going to come to the place where the tracks turned northward down into the wide arroyo.

His uppermost thought as he watched the riders getting closer, was what would happen when they halted to look down into the tangle of growth in the canyon, and were challenged by someone over yonder in the rocks.

It was not going to be like challenging everyday rangemen. He dried sweat off his palms and regripped the Winchester.

Now, as the sun sank in a blaze of saffron haze, Burton's men were passing the rocks across the way where watchers were probably scarcely even breathing.

Ash Duran was in the lead. Frank wondered if he was as tired as he should be, having been in the saddle last night and again today.

Ash was watching the tracks without having to lean to do it. Where the tracks turned down into the big arroyo, he settled against the cantle, left hand a little higher than the saddle horn, right hand resting on a saddle-swell, and rode only an additional forty or fifty yards, then halted. The men behind him came up and also drew rein.

Frank could not take his eyes off Duran. He saw him turn slightly, still loose in the saddle, speak to one of the other men, then raise his arm to gesture toward both rims, the one eastward, and the rim that was westerly. He was almost certainly saying they should split up with half riding one rim, the other men riding the opposite rim in order to be able to see down into the arroyo.

That fretting horse someone had left tethered down in the

area of the rocked-up spring whinnied again, louder this time. It had probably picked up the scent of strange horses in the southward distance.

Al Springer smiled and softly said, "Get set, boys," as he eased the saddle gun across the rough surface of his rock.

CHAPTER 17

Toward Nightfall

THE Burton men were silent and motionless after that horse whinnied far ahead and out of their sight in the arroyo. Frank made a guess. "They're wonderin' if they shouldn't try sneakin' down into the canyon."

He got no answer. Springer and Duncan were watching as Ash slackened his reins to ride. Clearly audible and flat-sounding, a voice, which seemed to come from everywhere or nowhere, called out.

"That's good, gents. Right where you are. Keep your hands up in plain sight."

It caught the riders flat-footed. Only one of them moved. His head was twisted westerly in the direction of the rocks as he leaned suddenly to grip the booted carbine under his *rosadero*.

There were two gunshots, both pitched high. Ash Duran was hit twice, once from whoever had fired over yonder and also by Albert Springer in the opposite direction. Before the echoes passed and within seconds of the time required for Duran to leave his saddle and hit the ground, Springer sang out. The riders swung heads in this new direction.

"One down, five to go. Who wants to be second?"

Frank turned his head. Springer was curled into the stock of his old Winchester with his weathered face set like granite. He had the hammer back and his finger curled inside the trigger guard. He was emotionless—as steady as a rock.

One of the riders raised his voice. He was clearly unwilling to do anything. Perhaps the discovery that he and his companions had ridden into an ambush, were out in the open while their ambushers were not visible among the rocks, convinced him that there were no acceptable odds, that there was no chance at all.

"All right," the rider called in a growly yell. "What do you want?"

The next order came from the opposite direction. Frank recognized Bud Shilling's voice. "Dump the hand guns—all of you. Fine. Now then, step down and step directly to the head of your horses. Don't even look at them carbines."

The horsemen obeyed. Frank looked at the former deputy marshal. Springer had neither raised his eyes from his gunsights nor eased up his crooked finger inside the trigger guard. But he was grinning.

The light was waning, although dusk would be a while arriving, and full darkness would be even longer this time of year.

One man Frank recognized came forth from the westerly rocks: Will Perkins, carrying his Winchester in both hands and walking carefully toward the horsemen without once taking his eyes off them. When he was close, he said something the watchers on the east side of the arroyo could not hear. But they heard that growly-voiced man's retort.

"We're not goin' to. How many fellers you got around here?"

Perkins did not reply. He grounded the saddle gun and pulled out his hand gun, cocked it and gave an order. The captives leaned to pull up trouser legs. Both Mexicans had wicked-bladed bootknives, and one of the other men had a little under-and-over belly gun with a bore big enough for a man to shove his finger into. They threw these weapons aside and straightened up.

Will gave another order. The remaining five riders got belly down in the dirt and pushed their arms straight out in front.

Finally, Albert Springer eased his hammer down very carefully, looked left and right, and got up to his feet. Kent Duncan and Frank Tennant followed him down the grassy slope. Across the way Will's gunhands were also leaving their rocks.

When Frank was close enough, he heard one of the prone men say, "I told him, damn it. I been tellin' him for the last five miles, an' all he said was, 'Look around—do you see any men or horses? In this open country there's no place for 'em to ambush us.'" The disgusted speaker gave a bitter grunt and twisted his head to look at the men coming from two directions.

Another prone man spoke, but this time loudly and pleasantly. *"Oh-yey, Francisco, qué pasa?"*

Frank met the sweaty, dark face with its white teeth showing in a broad smile and shook his head. "When are you goin' to quit, Rosario?"

The bulky Mexican rolled his eyes. "Maybe now. I think that man wants to shoot us."

Will Perkins gazed at the sweating *vaquero* with obvious scorn, and spat.

Bud Shilling went over the prone men for more hideout weapons, found none, and stepped back. Frank was kneeling beside Ash Duran. Both those Winchester slugs had hit him hard; either one would have killed him. Frank leaned on his carbine, gazing at the corpse, then slowly rummaged through both shirt pockets and arose holding the little golden locket. He opened it, snapped it closed, and faced around as Perkins prodded their prisoners to their feet.

They herded the prisoners ahead down into the arroyo, keeping well to one side and clear of underbrush. The two Mexicans led the horses. The younger one was very much afraid but Rosario Valdez wasn't. A long time ago before he had even acquired a horse, he had accepted a fatalistic philosophy. He would continue to ride, to breathe, to gamble and laugh and eat *entamotados* every chance he got, and when the day, or night, came when *el visitador* tapped his shoulder, Rosario Valdez would be ready.

This time he had briefly thought he had felt a little brush

of fingers across his sweaty shirt, but evidently that had been a slight breeze because he was still alive. When they reached camp near the stoned-up spring and the horses had been cared for, he helped Al Springer make a little fire and sat patiently silent until everyone was gathered around. Then he winked across at Frank Tennant.

Will Perkins rummaged for something to eat. There was enough to go around but just barely. The coffee gave out first but there was tobacco. One of the gringos, a dark man with a slit of a mouth like a bear trap, and hooded tawny-tan eyes, missed nothing. When Bud Shilling asked where Charles Burton was, it was this man who replied. The moment he spoke, Frank recognized the growly voice.

"Down at the yard as far as any of us know. He sent us out. Sent a couple of other parties out, farther north."

Perkins drained his cup and dropped it. "Which of you sons of bitches was in that ambush up by Guadalupe?"

The grim-faced man stared at Perkins. "What ambush?"

Albert Springer smiled as he reached around, hefted his carbine, faced forward, aimed it at the bleak-faced man's middle, and cocked it. "Ask him one more time," he said to Perkins.

One of the other men answered quickly. "Only him'n Ash. The rest of us was around the yard. We didn't know there'd been trouble until they come ridin' back on tucked-up horses."

Springer eased his finger back until it touched the trigger. Frank spoke quickly. "Why did Burton go up there?"

"Because some Mexican named Villalobos sent word by a little kid there'd been some shootin' up there. He said he didn't care about that but he wanted his money back. So he took a crew and rode up there."

Frank had another question. "Did he get the money?"

The frightened man bobbed his head under the bitterly disapproving stares of his companions. "Yeah, he got it from Ash. That Mexican come riding down to meet Mister Burton.

Told him sure as hell there'd be a posse hunting him. You know the rest, I expect."

For a long while there was silence as the men got comfortable on the ground, smoking and watching one another. Eventually Will Perkins stood up. Springer immediately did the same thing. While Perkins went among the saddles for a lass-rope, Springer gazed unblinkingly at the man with the menacing face and the bear-trap mouth. Not a word was spoken.

Frank sat cross-legged and stiff. He knew what was going to happen and he did not entirely disapprove—it was just that he had never been this close before when it had been done.

Springer and Perkins tied the coarse-faced man's hands in back and herded him northward away from the others. There was not a sound for a half hour as men strained to hear. Rosario Valdez drank deeply from someone's canteen and handed it to the younger Mexican, who could not have swallowed if he'd been dying of thirst.

Will and Springer returned without the lariat, said nothing, resumed their places at the little fire, and got comfortable before raising expressionless faces, looking from man to man, seeming to be awaiting reproach. There was none.

Shilling said, "Frank?" and when Tennant looked up the saloonman shrugged. "I expect we can figure we've settled up for Cord Bierk."

Springer spoke. "Naw. One man don't make an ambush, Bud."

Perkins looked from Frank to Bud Shilling before speaking. "Some of you fellers want to go back, you can. Me, I figure the only way to keep from havin' nits is to kill lice."

Shilling squirmed, the four remaining hard riders waited and watched. Whatever the posse men decided, the fate of the captives would have to be settled first; they did not expect to be taken along. There already was one dead man out there somewhere hanging from a tree.

But they were.

The moon was climbing, that faint fragrance that came to the desert at night was discernible, and except for the little flinty bits of rock mixed into the leached-out soil, the horsemen would have passed along soundlessly because no one spoke until they were ready to lope and the prisoners were warned about trying to make a run for it. Even if it had been fully dark, and it wasn't because of that nightrider's moon, there had never been a horse foaled that could outrun a bullet.

The moon was high, its light eerily diffused over an immeasurable breadth of country, before Frank held up an arm and dropped down to a walk. They had covered a lot of ground. From here on he knew the country—they were getting close.

For several hours he had been considering plans and rejecting them. The one he finally accepted was not what he would have voluntarily chosen, but it might work. He had an element of surprise in his favor. He hoped he had anyway. It was late.

He showed them where to tie the horses, then told the captives to get belly down again. This time they bound them securely and shoved bandannas into their mouths, and also cautioned them against making any noise. Rosario Valdez rolled his eyes when Frank came to gag him. "*Loco, compañero*," he said, speaking in rough border-Spanish. "You were very lucky the other time. You can't do it twice."

Frank shoved in the gag, tied it, cuffed his old friend on the back, and arose to grin and wink. Valdez rolled his eyes again, which was all he could do.

Albert Springer came over to Frank shaking his head. "We got to leave someone here with the horses. If those fellers get loose they'll run 'em off an' we'll be caught from in back as well as in front."

They left a man.

The walk was not long, about a half mile. Long before

they detected the smell of cattle, they could make out buildings, some larger than others, all placed in a rough horseshoe shape around an area of dowdy old cottonwood trees. The yard was large; it was also dusty. Where they stopped to look and listen, if it had not been for their spurs they would not have made a sound.

Frank pointed to the bunkhouses first, then at the rambling main house with its covered porch along the entire front. Will Perkins reached inside his shirt to scratch as he said, "The house is yours, Frank. Rest of us'll get set to settle up with anyone who comes out into the yard if there's trouble."

Springer regarded Will Perkins almost with affection. "I got to hand it to you, saloonman," he said quietly. "You think like a renegade."

Perkins turned slowly to regard Springer. Frank thought he would say something but he didn't; he instead jerked his head and led the way through ghostly moonlight, leaving Frank alone.

He approached the house as he had done before, by going southward until he was behind it, then very cautiously approaching the porch which was only half covered; the rest of it had no overhanging roof.

Where it was covered, moonglow did not reach. He got up there next to the door and put his head against the wood. There was not a sound. He hadn't expected one this late at night.

The other time he had not gotten inside by the door, but by a rear window that had a badly warped frame. If his uncle had figured out how he had entered the first time, he would have devised some way to bar that window. There was an iron latch, but it could not be forced closed because of the extensive warping.

Frank eased along on tiptoe, reached the window, leaned his carbine aside, and gently felt the wood. It was slivery, cracked, and bowed. He leaned from one side to look in.

Because it was darker in the house than it was outside, he could make out only one object, an old chair covered with dust, which had been in the same place his last time back here.

He tested the window. It had opened only partway before, then the warping bound it. The same thing happened now. He had been able to barely squeeze through before and did not risk making noise by forcing it open any more this time.

The house smelled of stale air mixed with tobacco smoke. Getting past the half-open window was difficult, but he made it without making any more noise than could have been heard by someone in the room, and there was no one. This was a storeroom: there were old crates, some newer ones, and upon a little table where a coal oil lamp stood, there was a gold scale complete with graduated weights.

Except for three or four crates without dust on them, everything in the room had been here before. He closed the window very carefully, forcing it to remain wedged, then moved toward the closed door.

His eyes were adjusting. It was very dark in the room. With the door partially opened, visibility improved a little.

He knew where his uncle's office was. Against the east wall of the office stood that steel safe he had opened before.

But first he had to know where his uncle was. If he was in his bedroom, then Frank's choices were limited to only one— he had to overcome his uncle, tie and gag him before returning to the office.

For a long moment he stood in the gloomy corridor gauging the night, the interior of the house, his chances of doing what Rosario Valdez had said could not be done twice.

He went toward Burton's bedroom on tiptoes. The door was closed. He tested the latch very gently. It was one of those latches that by squeezing a thumb-pad-sized lever on the outside lifted the little bar from its hanger on the inside. The trick was not to exert too much pressure, or when that little bar came up it would do so rapidly and strike the metal top of the latch.

He had to wipe a sweaty palm on his trouser leg before touching the thumb-pad plate. He was very careful as he put pressure on the latch.

It began to rise. He could feel the inside bar coming up. It only had to rise about an inch to clear the hanger. When he thought it was high enough, he used his other hand to push gently on the door.

Handmade hinges of hammered steel that did not seat well and which had probably never been oiled, ground harshly. The noise was audible all over the house.

Frank cursed under his breath, pushed hard to get inside swiftly, and stopped a yard past the opening, looking into the barrel of a six-gun in his uncle's right hand. Evidently the hinge noise had warned Burton in plenty of time to reach for his bedstand weapon and swing his feet to the floor.

Frank had just learned something about his uncle. He was a very light sleeper.

They were separated by about eight or ten feet. Beyond his uncle in the log wall was a window. It allowed the only light to enter the room. The window was closed and barred from the inside, and although its glass was dirty and wavery, it let in enough moonlight for each man to recognize the other one.

There was a faint fragrance in the room.

CHAPTER 18

Settling Scores

THE events, which occurred almost simultaneously, happened very fast. First, the woman screamed as she jerked half upright behind his uncle in the bed, then his uncle fired.

The noise was deafening, the bullet hit the doorlatch, sending bits of metal in all directions. The woman was lunging in panic to get out of the bed. Her frantic movement had made Burton miss.

Frank stepped right as he was drawing. Burton roared a curse at the terrified woman who was making his edge of the bed pitch and twist. This time the gunshots were so close together they sounded like one extremely loud explosion.

Frank thumbed back and let the hammer fall a second time. Charles Burton was already tumbling toward the floor. He lost the hand gun. The second slug hit him high in the side with enough impact to literally boost him into the air and dump him against a small table with two glasses and a whiskey bottle atop it. The bottle spilled, the glasses broke, the table fell across Charles Burton who was on his left side with his head flung back.

Tennant's ears were ringing. On the far side of the bed, with moonlight backgrounding her through the window, the woman stood rigidly with both hands pressed against her mouth, staring at the dead man. She was Mexican with long, thick black hair.

Frank stood with the gun hanging at his side. He took a couple of steps and kicked the gun Burton had dropped. It skidded under the bed. He looked at the woman. She was staring at him with huge, round eyes. He said, "It's all right. You stay in here. Don't come out. You understand?"

149

She nodded, still pressing both hands over her mouth. He walked out of the room and down the hall to his uncle's office.

He was able to see fairly well despite the darkness. This room too smelled of tobacco smoke. He was kneeling at the safe when all hell broke loose out in the yard. He wasted no time working the dial on the safe. The battle in the yard sounded like a genuine war, then silence returned as suddenly as it had been shattered.

Frank hauled back the door, saw his saddlebags with an enormous sense of relief, draped them over a shoulder, and arose. He was in the corridor again before it occurred to him to raise the flaps and make sure his money was in there. It was. He rebuckled the three tie-downs, reslung the bags over his shoulder, and went directly to the rear door, lifted its heavy oaken *tranca*, looked both ways first, then stepped out. His carbine was leaning where he had left it.

Out in the yard someone yelled. His reply was another fusilade of bullets. The surprised men in their huts had no idea who was firing at them each time they attempted to rush out after the shooting at the main house, but they had learned one thing—whoever it was knew how to set up an ambush. Every time one of Burton's men tried to ease a door open, bullets came. There were three corpses lying in the yard. By moonlight they had a demoralizing effect on men who had rushed forth half asleep, straight into a wall of lead. The survivors who had fled back to shelter were wide awake.

Frank slipped to the southwest corner of the main house from in back, peeked around, heard terrified horses charging round and round in a corral, and sprinted for the cover of a well house. From there he looked and listened, but there were no echoes and nothing to be seen. Burton's hired hands could have been brave men, but the fact that they were unwilling to make another blind charge against invisible gunmen proved that they were not fools either.

Frank got all the way around behind several outbuildings

to the corral with the terrified saddle animals in it, flung the gate wide, and after the horses had fled, half choking from their dust, he yelled loudly, "I got it!" and turned away from the yard heading out where their horses were.

He had gone no more than five yards when a blinding explosion brightened the entire yard for two or three seconds. A rush of hot wind brushed against him. It had a powerful odor. He stood looking back. When darkness returned it seemed darker than before.

He heard running men, ragged footfalls passing south of where he stood. Once, a complaining voice sounding breathless, said, "We run a mile. Those horses wasn't this far."

Bud Shilling.

Frank turned parallel with the runners and hurried along too.

The posse man they'd left with the horses was down on one knee, Winchester to his shoulder, but when he heard Springer reply to the harness maker, he eased the weapon aside and stood up in immense relief. Springer said, "You ain't run in fifteen years, but you sure as hell better do it now."

When Frank came up, the guard was already freeing the horses. The others swarmed around him, anxious to get away. A croaking noise from the ground stopped Frank. Rosario Valdez's cheeks were puffed out like bellows. Frank knelt, yanked the gag down, and Valdez's words tumbled out. "What did you do—have dynamite?"

The others were mounted. Kent Duncan called, "Frank, you're makin' us waste time."

Tennant wasted another moment freeing the arms of his old companion, then sprang ahead, vaulted across leather, and followed the others. Duncan was leading. His course was steadily northwest in the direction of Guadalupe. Riding directly, without deviations, they could make very good time. The animals were rested.

When they slackened off an hour later, every one of them

twisted to look back. There was a fire raging in Burton's yard. Frank settled forward. "What the hell was that explosion?"

Perkins leveled a rigid finger at the harness maker. "He done it. There was a crate of dynamite sticks in the storehouse across the yard. He grabbed one as we were runnin' to get into position. I saw him take it."

Shilling looked around. No one was smiling. In fact every one of them was still shaken. Shilling spoke defensively. "What was wrong with that?"

Kent glared at him. "You could have warned us."

Bud glared back. "How? I didn't even know where you were. What'd you want me to do—yell out that I had some dynamite?"

They rode doggedly for several yards with Bud glaring at them before he spoke again. "I wasn't goin' to throw it until I heard Frank yell. I figured if I flung it then, as we was tryin' to get away from there, it'd stun those bastards into stayin' inside until we got plumb away. Anythin' wrong with that?"

There wasn't anything wrong with it. In fact it was a minor stroke of genius, but to men who had been sweating like stud horses during the battle and who had been shaken down to their boots when the damned world seemed to blow up in their faces, it would be a while before anyone told Bud Shilling he'd had a good idea.

Eventually, with many miles behind them and no sign of pursuit, Albert Springer laughed. It was an out-of-place sound. "Did you throw that thing at one of the bunkhouses, Bud?"

"No. I threw it so's it'd fall short of a bunkhouse. I didn't want to make a damned massacre."

Springer turned to Frank. "What happened at the house?"

He told them. They mulled it over for a few miles before Duncan said, "Y'know, Frank, a man don't deserve to be that lucky. Suppose he hadn't had that woman in bed with him?"

"He'd have shot me sure as hell. I didn't have a chance the way he was aiming that gun at me."

"See? That's what I mean. Someone's lookin' out for you."

Perkins was buttoning his old coat to the gullet as he squinted upward where the moon had been. It was gone now, which meant the night was well advanced. He already knew that because it was getting cold. "We got to rest these animals directly," he muttered, but made no move to implement his statement.

There was something sticking Frank in the chest. He draped the saddlebags across his lap, opened the shirt, and groped for what he thought would be a sliver. It was indeed a sliver. It was a shard of steel from the door latch that had been shattered by his uncle's gunshot. It was about five inches long, jagged, and very sharp.

It had struck the big golden rosary first, losing its momentum, then it had bent. The bent part was what had been rubbing Frank.

He worked the sliver loose, felt its tip, which was dagger sharp, pulled out the crucifix to see where the steel had imbedded itself, rebuttoned his shirt over the crucifix, and rode for a considerable distance holding the steel sliver. If the crucifix had not been there, the sliver would have gone straight into his chest about where his heart was. Five inches of razorlike steel would have done what Burton's bullet had not done.

He pocketed the sliver, did not mention any of this to his companions, and when they eventually climbed down to blow the horses, he listened to the others as they recounted what had happened back yonder, and studied the flawless sky with its tiers of winking, pure white stars.

They made two more rest halts before cold predawn perceptibly brightened the land in an eerie way, had rooftops in sight as the sun popped up over the dim curve of the world, and rode at a flat-footed walk straight for Duncan's livery barn.

It was cold. There was not a word said as they cared for their animals, helped by the big-eyed but silent hostler, and went out front to pause in shadows gazing up the empty roadway.

Duncan said, "Damned cafe won't be open for another hour." That seemed to be as good a way to end things as any. Without more talk they broke up heading in different directions. Duncan turned back down into his barn. Bud Shilling struck out for the lean-to off the back of his harness works where he lived.

Frank walked up to the dark jailhouse, booted Winchester under his arm, saddlebags over his shoulder. It was warmer inside the old building than it was outside, and that big blond man who had been acting as town marshal was not there, so Frank dumped his weapon and saddlebags on the desk, took down the cell-room keys, and went down where it was still dark to open one cell. Jorge Medina was awake, but across the narrow corridor the last of the Durans was snoring.

They went up to the office. Frank lighted the coal oil lamp, hung it from its ceiling hook, and said, "Sit down, Jorge."

He was still talking when sounds of Guadalupe coming to life outside the jailhouse were noticeable inside. When he had said it all, he picked up the booted carbine, the saddlebags, opened the door, and jerked his head for Medina to precede him.

As they trudged across the roadway into shadows that still covered the east side of town and went down through a dog trot to Mex town, the handful of people who were abroad stared.

Antonia was out back brushing a long-legged, thorough-bred-looking bay horse when they saw her. Frank recognized his horse. When Antonia whirled, saw them and ran toward them, Frank spoke shortly to her father. "That's my horse. She must have taken it out of the public corrals. Duncan's goin' to have a fit. He'll think someone stole it."

Medina opened his arms as he said, "Later—we'll take care

of that later." Antonia hurled against him; he had to brace. Over her head Medina winked at Frank as he said, "We are very hungry and tired men, *dulce*. Maybe this afternoon when we have slept . . ."

She leaned back looking upward through tears, then freed herself and went more slowly to Frank. They stood looking at one another, he warily, she with a flushed face and trembling lips. She stood on tiptoes and kissed him squarely on the mouth.

Her father blinked, then cleared his throat and turned his back on them as he strode toward the house and disappeared inside.

Frank dug out the little locket. "Thank you. It's the nicest gift I ever got."

She groped for a small handkerchief and while drying her eyes she said, "I wanted you to remember . . . I just didn't think you would ever come back. Why should you? The daughter of a harness maker—a Mexican."

He winced, then scowled, not at her but at the locket in his hand. "Don't say things like that." He carefully put the locket back into his pocket and raised his eyes to her face. She was truly beautiful. "I would have come back." He paused, took her hand, and squeezed it as they started toward the house. "I didn't expect for it to be this soon, for a fact."

"Frank, what happened to your face? Who did it?"

He smiled gently. "Let's not talk about it. It's over now."

"What happened?"

They were nearing the doorway when her father's voice reached them. "Where is breakfast, Antonia?"

She freed her hand and entered the house briskly. "Be patient. I'll get it."

Frank was staring at her when Medina turned to say something, saw the look on the younger man's face, turned back slowly and sat down at the table. He heaved a big, soft sigh.